The Missed Call of My Life

The Missed Call of My Life

Raj Sinha

PARTRIDGE

A Penguin Random House Company

To order additional copies of this book, contact
Partridge India
000 800 10062 62
orders.india@partridgepublishing.com

www.partridgepublishing.com/india

Contents

Acknowledgements

I'd like to thank:

- God especially Lord Shiva for his love and blessings.
- My late mother Noor Fatima for her unconditional love.
- My family especially my sisters Shabnam and Shailja for their constant support throughout my life.
- My first few readers Rajshree, Luv, Amit, Arpita, Sonia and Neha for their honest feedbacks on the manuscript.
- Ajay for his expertise in creating the cover photo.
- My childhood friends Sujit, Rohit, Prashant, Manu, Dipto, Nayier, Linu and others for being the most amazing friends' one could think of.
- My colleagues especially Disha, Gopal *jee*, Vishal *(baba)*, Ronny, Amar, Chandan, Heena, Charu and others for their continuous encouragement.

- Tushar, Scharolyn and Steve for being the best Managers I ever worked with
- Dhiren from WordsWay for proofreading the manuscript
- Bloody Good Books for providing platform for budding authors to showcase their talents
- Last but not the least I would like to thank Vandana who made this novel a reality.

With that, I'd like to welcome you to The Missed Call of My Life.

We Guest's Entrance Gate

'How may I help you?' the guard at the entrance gate greeted with a broad smile.

'I'm here for my full and final settlement,' I replied, trying my best to match his enthusiasm, however, hiding my face with a handkerchief.

'Do you have the pink slip?' the guard shot at me.

This time his tone was stern as he became suspicious of my unusual action. Though it was a cloudy day I was still trying to conceal my face. I could see his pearl white teeth shining. I wondered which toothpaste brand he used. Any toothpaste company would hire him to advertise their brand and here he was doing the job of a security guard.

I was aware of the fact that without the pink slip my entry in the premises was not possible so my obvious answer was, 'Yes, I have it.'

I pulled out my wallet and started looking for the pink slip, but to my horror it was not there. I started to panic, thinking I might have left it in my room.

The very thought of travelling back for an hour and that too in a DTC bus brought sweat on my forehead. The condition of our public transport can be compared with the population explosion in our country. These days travelling by bus is like going on a war. No matter how well you are dressed, once you are out, it looks like you have just ended a grueling wrestling match.

My fear was apparent on my face and the guard noticed it.

'Without the pink slip, I won't let you enter,' he declared.

I could envisage him being one of the guards from hell as shown in some mythological movies, only larger-than-life moustaches and broad eyebrows were missing.

I was convinced that before leaving the room I'd kept it in my wallet but somehow it was not there. When in stress you tend to imagine all sorts of things, and I being no exception to the rule started doubting my childhood friend Rohit, who coincidentally was my room partner too.

'He might have misplaced it but, then his area of interest was always the money kept in my wallet: he never ever touched any other documents, so he was all clear,' I pondered.

Now the only culprit left to blame was me. 'Shit!'

It was all I could manage to utter as I reluctantly moved my hands towards the hip pocket. Suddenly I felt a piece of paper: as I pulled out the paper it turned out to be the pink slip, *the* elusive pink slip. Trust me, it felt better than attaining orgasm.

'Here's my pink slip,' I grinned as I handed over my prized possession to him.

The guard was miffed by my reply and I could easily feel the heat while being frisked by him. The way he ran his electronic gadget all over my body especially to and fro over my private parts made me a bit uncomfortable yet I had no option but to go through it. Whether it was intentional or not was best left to one's imagination. Now I can imagine why famous Indian personalities make such a hue and cry while being frisked at international airports, especially in the US. Today I can easily relate to their plight as I myself had become one of the sufferers of indecorous frisking.

Soon the torture ended and I was allowed to enter the premises. As I was about to enter the premise a harsh voice halted my advancing steps, I do remember the voice, it was the guard from hell, sorry from the gate, once again.

'Now what else does he need from me?' I thought.

'Sir, for full and final settlement you need to take the other way. Let me guide you,' he offered and started walking in the opposite direction.

I was flabbergasted by his reply because it'd been over a year since I worked in We Guest and I knew that this was the only entry gate the company had. We reached the left side of the building which was mostly reserved for guards. Before I could utter anything he pushed a door at the end. I could see the stairs going downwards towards the basement with lights streaming out.

I stepped down slowly as I wasn't sure, hoping that I hadn't hurt his ego too much by showing the elusive pink slip and it wasn't a trap of strangling me to death by his pals in the basement. All my fears evaporated the moment I reached the basement and turned left. It turned out to be a familiar place. During our training days, this place used to be our leisure room. This was the corner most room located in the basement along with the other training rooms.

When we were in training we were not allowed to go beyond a certain point, and now I knew the reason why. This place was reserved for ex-employees who'd come for their full and final settlement.

Once you leave the company you become a cast-off and are looked upon as a leper. Even the guards won't give you a second look, I thought.

As I was deep in my thoughts a sweet voice brought me back to reality.

'Are you here for your full and final settlement?' she enquired.

I turned towards her expecting her face to be as sweet as her voice but to my disappointment her looks were no match for her voice.

'Yes,' I responded.

'Ah…sorry, then you will have to wait for a while as the concerned person would be a bit late,' she informed me apologetically.

'OK, no problem, I'll wait,' I answered, forcing a smile.

I didn't want to stay long in the premises but it appeared as if luck was not on my side so I reluctantly grabbed the corner most seat. Even though the receptionist was not attractive she had big boobs. She must have been a new joinee otherwise I'd have noticed her for sure. It was hard to believe that I'd left this place. I became nostalgic as it appeared that it was only yesterday when I joined We Guest and wanted to spend the rest of my professional life in this organization. But my journey in the company met an abrupt end.

Maybe it was all destiny, I sighed.

In between all this, I forgot to introduce myself.

Hi All, my name is Shiv, lanky, slender. I'm a 25-year-old guy from Patna, the capital of Bihar. An average-looking fellow. OK, you can say below average, I'll accept.

My journey from a small town to this metro had been a roller-coaster journey. To know about my journey you just have to skim through these pages and I'll try my best to keep you entertained.

From Patna to New Delhi

(Time: 8 a.m. at the breakfast table)

'Have you checked your CA results?' my father asked as I was about to take my first bite of toast. I expected the question coming my way but somehow the timing was not right. My father should have waited till we ended our breakfast.

Now how hard you try, one can't go against one's destiny. I had to answer him. I knew the result as I'd already checked it the previous night and the only time a student hides his results is when he's flunked. Otherwise, yelling over the loudspeakers even to strangers would be normal.

He guessed my results simply by looking at my fretful face.

'So, you have failed *again*!' he said, emphasizing the word 'again'.

'Y…yes,' I replied still holding the French toast. All hell broke loose as soon as I declared the results.

'Do you know where all of your friends have reached today?' He asked in an agitated tone.

This is the problem with today's parents: the moment they come to know about their children's failure they start comparing them with their successful friends. I really don't know what's the purpose of dragging your fruitful friend's name in the conversation. Maybe the objective is to make you feel even more guilty.

The sad part is that nobody wants to talk about those who remained failures like me.

In situations like these you want the earth beneath you to cave in and you want to jump inside. But this was not the Ramayan and I was not enacting the role of Sita so nothing like that happened.

'I really don't know what you will do with your future. I just give up.' He raised his hand in despair.

Somebody has truly said that success has many fathers but failure has none. At the moment my father wanted to abandon me for my failure.

I was listening with my head lowered still holding my toast thinking when I'd get a chance to eat it as I was starving. I had already sacrificed my dinner the previous night because of the results. I didn't want to miss my breakfast now.

I wished whether sacrificing food could help one to pass or to get additional marks in an examination. I wondered how much food we could save especially in India where parents are after their children's lives. This way we can resolve two major challenges: one, food shortage, and the other, bloodthirsty—sorry—results-thirsty parents.

On hearing the scolding my mother rushed from the kitchen to do damage control.

'Please control yourself, give him another chance, he would do well this time,' she said, as she would check my papers the next time. The typical Indian mother who always gets trapped between father and son but always fails to control either.

'He won't do anything. I can write that on a plain paper,' he declared as if he was ready to give Bejan Daruwalla, the famous astrologer, a run for his predictions.

Though I was starving but I'd had enough food in the form of scolding at the breakfast table so I decided to leave on an empty stomach. I knew that I was working very hard but was somehow unable to clear my exams by just a few marks. Maybe I was not destined to be a CA professional. This time I'd missed it by a meager four marks. I tried to soothe myself by blaming the Almighty but the reality was that I had failed once *again*.

As I was busy in self-assessment my cell phone rang.

It was Rohit, my childhood friend. We had been friends since Class Four. He was currently working in a call centre situated in NOIDA. He too had tried and burnt his fingers to clear CA exams but after two failed attempts he decided to let it go. Now he was content working in a call centre and earning a respectable salary. In the past he had asked me to join him, but somewhere I wanted to keep burning my fingers. Maybe it was self-belief that one day I'd become a successful CA. But it was proving to be a tough nut. He had assured me that he'd get me employed in his call centre without much worry.

After much reluctance I picked the call.

'Hey Rohit, how are you? How's life?' I asked trying to hide my remorseful state.

'I'm fine; just called to remind you that you have to collect my pass certificate from college as I have to show the original certificates here,' he gave the reason for the call.

'Don't worry, I'll collect it,' I assured him.

'May I ask something?' I hesitantly asked him.

'Yes, of course.' I replied.

'Are there any current openings in your call centre?' I enquired.

'So you've failed once again?' he asked sheepishly

I hadn't expected him to come to that conclusion so rapidly but it seemed that he was keeping track of the CA results even though he'd left it quite a while back.

'Bastard!' I thought.

'Yes, I have,' I replied straightforwardly. There was no point concealing the truth.

'Now it's enough. I want to join your call centre. Is it possible?' I enquired.

He paused for a few seconds and replied.

'Pack your bags and come here. I'll take care of the rest.'

'Thanks buddy, I'll be there in a week's time,' I replied.

'Fine. See you in Delhi, brother,' he wound up.

It felt like a hefty burden being taken off my shoulder. Now it was time to announce my future plan to my father. I returned to the dining room where my dad was watching his all-time—or say anytime—favorite programme, the news. The current news topic was whether Shahid Kapoor and Kareena Kapoor would ever get back together or not.

'So, have you decided what you would do now?' my father demanded the moment he saw me.

'Yes, I have,' I replied assertively.

The news anchor was shouting his lungs out in the background. I wondered whether there was any connection between our decisions or not. My reply was like a arrow to him which could be easily seen on his face.

'What…?' he said.

'Yes, I have decided. I will leave CA and will go to Delhi. I will work in the same call centre where Rohit works. The salary is good. I will stay with him for now. I'll look for alternative accommodation later,' I answered in one breath.

He didn't utter a single word and just looked at my face. Maybe he was too shocked to react. After five minutes of silence he finally spoke.

'So, when are you planning to go?' he asked, softening his tone.

It seemed that now he was totally convinced that CA or any competitive exam was not my cup of tea and accepted my decision. Finally, his dream of seeing his only son clearing any professional course or getting any lucrative government job had met a cruel end. Now he had to spend the rest of his life being the father of a call centre employee and not of any district magistrate.

'By the end of this week,' I replied.

'OK,' he responded as he turned back his attention to the news.

I returned to my room and fell on my bed. I could see my CA books lying on the shelf. Somewhere I was feeling ashamed looking at them as I was not able to take the best advantage of them. I felt like crying.

However, it was a momentous day for me as I had taken an important decision about my future.

The First Day in New Delhi

'Where the hell are you?' I screamed the moment Rohit picked up my call.

'I'm stuck in a traffic jam. Have you reached the station?' he enquired, sounding quite frustrated.

'Well, I've reached New Delhi and am waiting on platform number 16.'

'It'll take another 15–20 minutes for me to reach there,' he said.

'In the meantime you can do one thing: just get out from the station towards the Ajmeri Gate side and wait for me at the prepaid auto booth,' he directed.

'But make sure you reach there soon; you know I'm new to this place. 'I said

'Don't worry,' he assured me.

I was standing in the New Delhi Railway station where people from all parts of the country come in hope of better jobs and lives, and I was one of the immigrants. It didn't take long for me to come out of the station, courtesy various signboards.

I smelled the air of Delhi. I saw people who seemed to be from different backgrounds moving in and out of the station, including a few foreigners standing at a corner looking as amused as I was.

I wondered how they managed to carry such heavy luggage. With such stamina they could easily have surpassed our Indian weightlifters. I had just two bags and still was literally pooped carrying them. Soon I was standing outside trying to locate the prepaid auto booth as instructed by Rohit.

Suddenly I saw this attractive lady approaching me with a smile on her radiant face. I was confused whether that smile was for me or for somebody else, so I turned around, but no one was standing there.

It had never happened with me that a girl even half as lovely as her had approached me this way. I speculated that maybe she was confused, and my face resembled that of someone known to her. So I smiled back at her, thinking of my chances to date her in future.

'Hi!' she greeted.

'He…hello,' I replied timidly.

'It seems there's some misunderstanding…' I sputtered. In no time she took out a small Indian flag and pinned it on my shirt.

'Now what is this for? Am I not looking like an Indian?' The very thought went through my mind.

Soon I got the answer to my question, as she demanded Rs. 50.

'What for?' I questioned.

'For this,' she responded, pointing to the flag.

'Well, don't you think Rs. 50 is a bit too much for this,' I asked.

'Well, it's our national flag and pride, so in that sense Rs. 50 is nothing,' She repeated her parroted lines which I was sure that she must have said umpteen times in the past.

There was no point arguing. It was better to pay the price for one's own imprudence, so I handed over Rs. 50 to her.

'Thank you, *Bhaiya*,' she grinned.

After being duped of Rs. 50 her smile was needling me like a cactus, but at least she could have done better by not calling me *bhaiya*!

What a start: I was tricked within an hour of reaching Delhi. I promised myself right there that I'd never smile back at strangers, specially the opposite sex. Somebody has truly said that smiles can be deceptive at times. I slowly moved towards the prepaid auto booth feeling embittered.

I had seen news about the Delhi Metro Rail and how it had become the lifeline of Delhites in a short time. It was my first opportunity to look at the Metro construction going on in full swing near the New Delhi Railway Station. I was busy in my thoughts when somebody patted my back.

It was Rohit.

At first glance, I couldn't recognize him. He had changed a lot, and for the better. Whether it was Delhi or his job which had brought this transformation, I was not sure. A guy who was always dressed in simple formal clothes was now wearing a trendy tee and jeans. Reebok sports shoes had now taken the place of traditional Bata sandals. Short, crew-cut hair stood straight up due to his overuse of hair gel.

A bracelet on one wrist, and I could even notice an earring in his left ear. It was a complete makeover in just six months. Truly commendable!

'Hello buddy,' he greeted and gave me a tight hug.

'Yes brother, long time,' I replied.

'I know you have umpteen questions about my transformation, but first let's get to my room; I'll explain there,' he said as he picked up my bag.

'Yes, I *would* like to know, and now I know the reason why you haven't visited your own home town,' I winked.

He gave a sly smile as we both moved towards his bike.

Soon we were heading towards his room. Delhi is a giant city. It was my first visit since I was 8–9 years old, when I last visited this place. I still remember a few places which I had visited then, like India Gate, CP, the Delhi Zoo and *Appu Ghar*, the usual tourist destinations of Delhi then. But there was one thing which made a long-lasting impression on me, and that was visiting an automated milk booth. I know I may sound like a backward person but to imagine getting milk from a machine was unbelievable for a guy like me. Since my childhood I was used to watching the milkman trying his best to squeeze the milk out of the teats, and if the cow was cranky, it could be downright dangerous. The cow might even pee in your face. But there were no such problems here. You just needed to insert a coin, and you'd get the milk in a container. As a kid, my enthusiasm could be matched to Neil Armstrong's landing on the moon.

'So, how was your journey?' Rohit asked me.

'Nothing special—except for the two ladies in my compartment.' I replied.

'What?' Rohit jammed the brakes. I almost tripped but somehow managed to grab his T-shirt at the last moment.

'Easy, Rohit, I could have fallen,' I yelled.

'Having spent your journey with two females, aren't you feeling lucky!' he ribbed me.

'Chill, don't get excited. Let me finish. The first one was a year old, a never-ending wailing toddler, and the second one was her grandmother.'

'The toddler cried the whole night, and when she finally slept, we reached New Delhi station,' I grumbled.

'It was an atrocious experience which I suffered during the entire journey.'

Rohit roared with laughter. Thank God I didn't share the flag incident otherwise he'd have died laughing. He kick-started his bike and we were off towards his room again.

Thanks to the colossal traffic jams it took us approximately an hour to reach his rented accommodation in Shakarpur in East Delhi. Once I reached his room I took a shower, had lunch, and relaxed on his bed.

We decided to converse about the job the next day. I was too tired, and didn't know how long I was going to sleep. Rohit's room was on the second floor. I didn't know when, but I felt as if the bed was shuddering. Maybe it didn't like my scent or weight, or it was an earthquake.

The moment I realized that it was an earthquake I just hopped out of bed and started running towards the door.

'Run, run, Rohit, it's an earthquake,' I screamed as I was heading down.

'Shh...listen...' Rohit wanted to say something, but I didn't want to die on my first day in Delhi. I was out in the open and as I was gasping for oxygen, I realized that it was only me who was standing alone.

'Do they all want to die?' I thought as it seemed as if the earthquake had fizzled out.

I was standing in only my pajamas, and people were gawking at me from their balconies.

'Who's this idiot?' somebody shouted.

'Ahh…I'm sorry, he's new,' Rohit said in an embarrassed voice.

'This idiot just wanted to save your life and rather than thanking me you are abusing me,' I wanted to retort, but kept quiet.

Something was wrong. Was I dreaming? No, I felt shaking of the bed but still nobody came out, I was introspecting.

'Are you alright?' Rohit asked me as he grasped my hand.

'Yes, it seems the earthquake is over,' I replied, wiping sweat from my forehead.

'That was not an earthquake.'

'But…I felt it,' I tried to explain.

'Did you hear anything else?' he quizzed.

'You mean that somebody was deliberately doing it?' I asked.

'No, idiot. Come, I'll explain,' he said, quickly moving into the building. I joined him on the stairs, not wanting any more humiliation from the neighbours.

'You didn't even listen to me and ran out,' he said as we walked into our room.

What did he mean? In these situations normal people have a tendency to run for their lives and not wait for instructions and get their asses crushed under the rubble, I thought.

'Now can you explain…?' I demanded.

'There is a railway track next to our building and whenever a train passes we do experience so-called earthquakes,' he grinned.

Now I realized that I'd heard something loud while stepping down.

'Sorry, brother, I forgot to inform you about it,' he said, trying to control his laughter.

'You bastard!' I yelled as I threw my sandal at him.

'It'll take some time for you to get adjusted to these changes,' he said, neatly gloving my sandal like a seasoned wicketkeeper.

We retired on our beds. I didn't know that my first day in Delhi would become so embarrassing for me. I prayed that none of my neighbours recognized me the next morning. And I dozed off.

The only concern I had was on how to differentiate between the rumbling of an earthquake and the one produced by trains running nearby. I was sure even Rohit couldn't answer that.

BPO Interview

The next day I woke up at 11 a.m. Rohit had taken an off that day. I wanted to visit the local area but due to the incident the previous night I decided to remain indoors. Soon, Rohit started preaching to me on how to crack the BPO interview.

'First of all, tell me what you think of a call centre or a BPO' he questioned.

'I guess it's like doing a job at night,' I replied with a grin.

'Anything else?' he probed.

'Fun, many female co-workers as compared to other sectors, parties and a handsome salary,' I replied.

'And the best part of it is, a complete transformation from a meek guy into a cool dude,' I continued with a wink.

'That's it?' he asked, sounding serious.

I started thinking of what to add to what I'd said. I recalled what I'd heard.

'Please don't mind, but a call centre job is not taken held in very high esteem in Indian society,' I murmured.

'Fuck them,' he said furiously. He didn't like the last part for sure.

Before I could say anything else Rohit started his version of 'The Call Centre'.

'Let me first clear your delusion. A call centre doesn't mean easy money, fun and no work. You have to really work hard to survive here. Commit one error and you are *out*. And it's not a joke to work at night. When most of your countrymen are sleeping, an annoyed customer can be chewing your head off. You will earn money, but every penny here will require more than 100 per cent of your effort. You will get to know this once you start working in this industry. Now about the females working here at night, it doesn't mean they are insipid. We forget that there must be a strong reason for working at night. Always remember the motto of call centre life is 'Work Hard, Party Harder'.

He spoke with the energy of somebody having had a knife jabbed in his chest. To be honest I was highly mesmerized by his speech.

'But what about the society?' I queried.

'The so-called society is overlooking one thing: if we didn't have call centres, just imagine the level of redundancy in India. Today these call centres are providing employment to thousands of people and giving them a chance to live an independent life. These call centres are also indirectly providing employment to thousands of others like cab drivers, guards, *dhaba* owners, and the list goes on. Not everyone can get through IIT or IIM, so stop thinking about the society. And I have one question for these society men: which sector would give you more than 20K with just a bachelor's degree?' he asked.

He had a valid point.

'I do agree,' I said.

'We can only hope that the perception will change in future.'

'Yes, I hope so,' I agreed.

However, the reality was that we were expecting something unattainable. It was like expecting Mahesh Bhatt to direct a mythological movie. In our present society a government peon has more importance than a call centre employee. We shifted our conversation to the practical aspects of call centres, specifically on how to crack a BPO interview.

'So, there are three simple rules for clearing a call centre interview,' he began.

'First, one should be comfortable with typewriting, Second, an elementary knowledge of English grammar, and third, for the personal interview you should be acquainted with 6–7 types of questions,' he continued.

'What type of questions?'

'It would be anything like: Introduce yourself; Why do you want to join a BPO; How long do you think we can expect you to be here; Do you have any plan for future studies; Hobbies, etc.,' he said.

'Don't worry, I have all the answers ready for you,' he said.

'For the introduction, it would be your birthplace, family background, and academic qualifications.

'On why you want to join a BPO, you just need to speak pleasant things like a vigorous environment, an opportunity to learn new skills, a handsome salary package, etc.

'For further studies, strictly say no plans. If you say yes, you are out. These people are not interested in your future studies,' he cautioned.

'On hobbies, it would be like watching movies, painting, writing, etc.,' he concluded.

After hearing his talk, it appeared as if it would be a cakewalk for me. I felt a bit relaxed. Well, it had been over three years since I started surfing on a computer, and just to elucidate, I didn't enroll for any computer classes. It's just that for the previous three years I had spent more time on Internet chatting—sex chats, to be precise—and surfing porn sites than anything else, so typewriting wouldn't be an issue. I was an average student in English, at least better than Rohit, so that too was not an impediment. So overall, it was not as problematic as I was expecting it to be.

'Before giving an interview in my company, why don't you try out some consultancy firm?' he advised.

'That's a good idea.' I agreed.

Though not on every occasion, but that day he was making sense.

'OK, there is this consultancy in Preet Vihar. Just visit them tomorrow, and see what transpires,' he recommended.

The entire conversation made me a bit overconfident, but I didn't know then that destiny had something else in store for me.

Interview I:
A Consulting Firm

I reached Sure Shot Consulting agency sharp at 10.00 a.m. as directed by Rohit.

Sure Shot Consultancy as the name advocates had an excellent track record—at least the sign outside the building stated so. 'We guarantee sure shot selection' was the tagline on the hoarding. It had a pretty lady's face displayed on the left hand side with a million-dollar smile. It seemed that the photographer had forced her to show all her teeth. She was wearing a headphone to display that she was a call centre employee. It made me feel good for two things: one that I would be getting a job for sure, and second, soon I would be interacting with pretty females like the one shown on the placard. I was standing in front of the reception greeted by an old lady there.

'Hello, how can I help you?' she asked.

'I am here for the call centre interview,' I responded.

'OK, have you got your CV?' she enquired.

'Yes, here it is,' I said as I handed over my CV. Probably it was one of the shortest CVs ever written in the professional world.

'OK, please fill this form in the adjacent room and wait for your turn,' she instructed.

I was taken aback the moment I stepped inside the room. It was almost jam-packed with other potential jobseekers. There were around 40–45 people with a male-female ratio of about 60:40.

I scanned the room for an empty seat. Though I'd have loved to be seated next to a female applicant but not a single seat was left empty beside a female. Even in serious situations like these we men don't want to miss an opportunity to be friends with the opposite sex. With no option left I sat next to a guy. Running through the form I saw that it consisted of general information such as salary expectations, prior experience if any, etc.

As I was about to start filling the form I heard a meek voice.

'Hi, I am Sundar, what's your name?' the guy next to me mumbled.

'Hello, I am Shiv,' I replied nonchalantly and continued filling up the form.

At first glance he looked like a bald goon with a full-grown beard from the Eighties movies so I was not very keen to talk to him.

'Is it OK if I talk to you?' he again asked timidly.

I could sense the nervousness in his tone, maybe because of the interview.

'No, that's OK,' I replied with a false smile.

'It's my first interview so I'm feeling a bit anxious. I just want to keep myself busy talking to someone,' he continued.

'It happens,' I retorted, sounding like an expert even though it was the first interview for me too.

It's human nature that some people tend to divert themselves by talking while others keep mum to keep anxiety away. The problem here was that I belonged to the second category. As I was already confident of getting a job in Rohit's company I was unperturbed, or you could say overconfident.

'Are you not feeling nervous?' he questioned.

'Nervous? Who, me?! Not at all,' I replied impudently.

'I am really scared for myself whether I would get selected or not,' he continued fearfully.

I could perceive his desperation by the increasing number of lines on his forehead.

'Don't worry, you will get selected,' I said, trying to boost his morale.

His actions made me feel pity for him though in his current state his chances of getting selected were like getting a one-in-a-million jackpot.

'What do you think about your chances?' he asked.

'Well, I don't see any reason why they will not select me,' I replied as I was cocksure about my chances.

'Here is my million dollars advice for you: it's just a BPO interview and not a rocket science interview, so just relax,' I said.

'Have faith in yourself and be poised. You will definitely cross this interview hurdle,' I concluded.

It seemed that this speech did have an effect on him as he stopped disturbing me and kept mum after that. I needed it badly as I had to finish filling up the form. Soon, I was done with the form and passed it over to the old lady at the reception and returned to my seat.

Sundar was still sitting there with both hands clutched together, head down and muttering something. Maybe he was reciting every prayer he had heard since his birth. His current state really made me feel sorry for him.

I quietly took my seat and started scanning the place.

The consultancy firm had just one big hall which was further or say smartly divided into four chambers by wooden partitions. There was a small passage in-between them. Within 10 minutes the same old lady at the reception area made an entry and announced my name. It seemed that she was playing the dual role of a receptionist-cum-peon.

'Who is Shiv?' she queried.

'It's me,' I replied, raising my hand. I didn't expect her to remember my face after all I was not Shahrukh Khan.

'Please follow me,' she said as she left the room.

'Best of luck,' I heard a meek voice, it was Sundar's.

'Thanks and the same to you,' I replied and followed the lady.

We reached the room at the end of the hall. It was relatively small as compared to others. There was a wooden table in the middle of the room with two chairs placed on the opposite sides. The lady asked me to have a seat. I was a bit skeptical whether she would be conducting the interview herself. Maybe she was playing a triple role here of receptionist, peon and now an interviewer as well.

'Well, who knows?' I thought.

As I was busy in my thoughts she herself revealed the suspense.

'Puja, our in-house interviewer, will be joining you in a minute to conduct a mock interview,' she explained.

'Mock interview?' I questioned.

'Yes, just to ensure that you are suitable for the final interview,' she grinned.

Now I knew the reason as to why my name was announced before those of the other candidates even though I had arrived much later. A soft voice intruded in my thoughts.

'Hi, I am Puja,' she introduced herself. 'I will be conducting the mock interview for you and based on your performance would give you the green signal for the final showdown.'

She was dusky, with sharp facial features. Her size-zero figure could give any model a run for her money. She was wearing a casual T-shirt as a top and tight-fitted jeans. The tagline on her T-shirt was, 'Born to Rule'. Not sure about others, but here she was about to rule whether I was fit for the final interview or not.

'Hello, I am Shiv. I am here for a BPO interview,' I introduced myself.

She conducted her interview by asking me exactly the same questions which Rohit had already trained me for the previous day. As I'd already mugged up my answers it didn't take me long to answer them. My interview lasted for exactly five minutes.

Her smile was an indication that I was fit enough for the final showdown.

'Congratulations, Shiv. You have cleared your mock interview. Please wait outside in the waiting area for your final interview,' she said.

It acted as a catalyst to my growing overconfidence. As I took my seat I noticed Sundar was not there. I was sure that he must have committed suicide by now. After 20 minutes I was asked to visit the room adjacent to the reception where the final showdown was going to take place.

I took a deep breath and knocked at the door.

'May I come in, please?' I asked.

'Yes, please,' somebody replied from inside.

'Thank you,' I replied as I entered the room.

'Please have a seat,' the lady sitting on the other side of the table told me.

Of all the rooms this was the most decked up. The chairs had comfortable cushions compared to the plastic chairs in the other room. This was the only room which had an air conditioner so I was feeling a bit cold. It seemed that all the superlative facilities were reserved for the visiting HR teams only and nobody cared for the poor candidates. It made sense: after all, the money was coming from these HR people only and not from the candidates. There were two people sitting opposite me forming the panel. One was female and the other was a male—or wait…a boy. Not sure, but he did resemble a 9th- or 10th-grade school boy. Maybe he had joined the call centre after his 10th exams.

Now the lady, she was easily one of the most exquisite girls I had ever seen. She was like a Bollywood actress who somehow was predestined to take my interview rather than dance seductively in the rain so that the hero could prove his masculinity by taking her to his bed. She had long curly hair, blue eyes, had applied red nail polish which I noticed while she was holding my CV in her hand.

At the moment my CV was luckier than me.

'Hi, I am Ravish and she is Ritu. We are from XYZ technologies. We are here to recruit for the voice processes,' the boy introduced himself and the prospective Bollywood queen. I was not at all interested in what he was saying; my whole concentration was on Ritu. I was wondering why Ritu was keeping mum. I wanted her to speak but it looked like it was being handled by Ravish only. I must mention that Ravish's accent was perfectly matching that of a US citizen. I felt like I was talking to an American rather than to an Indian.

'Hello, I am Shiv,' I introduced myself again.

'So, Shiv, before we start, please read this paragraph for us,' he told me as he handed over a piece of paper.

I was stunned as there was no introduction, no background details, nothing, just this piece of paper. I was not prepared for this. Since my school days I was one of the worst readers in my class. It used to give me goose bumps whenever I was asked to read something. My teacher used to constantly reprimand me for this. For reasons known to God alone, I was petrified of reading.

Suddenly my hands started trembling. Once you start losing your confidence it's very hard to get it back. I started to sweat even though the A/C was working at top speed. Due to my nervousness I perceived Ravish's face turning into one of my smile deprived English teacher who was always looking for an excuse to thrash me. With no option left, I slowly started reading the damn paragraph.

'Th...the...the...circu...circulation,' I fumbled.

I saw the grins which added more misery but somehow continued with the torture as I wanted to put an end to the embarrassment as soon as possible. It brought back the memory of my classmates laughing at me whenever I used to read. It took an endless five minutes to end the agony and straightaway I knew I had screwed it up big time. Soon I took control of the situation and wiped off the sweat from my forehead.

There was pin drop silence in the room. Maybe both of them were dumbstruck on hearing my speech. I really wanted to run away from this place but had to wait for the verdict.

I knew the final decision beforehand and as expected it was big NO in capital letters for me. I left the room with my head down. I was sure that the consultancy firm would even blacklist my name for future interviews. I felt like killing Rohit as he hadn't informed me about this scary reading part. As I was coming out I saw Sundar. I tried to ignore him but he had seen me.

'Hi Shiv,' he yipped.

'Oh hi, Sundar,' I replied acting as if I hadn't noticed him earlier.

'Thanks a ton!' he said beaming like Madhuri Dixit with her million dollar smile.

'For what?' I queried.

Don't tell me you got the job. I thought.

'I got the job and it's all because of you,' he said as he hugged me.

'What…how on Earth could he have got the job?' I almost tripped. 'Just moments ago he was wailing and now he had an appointment letter in his hand. Fuck,' I thought.

'Because of me…? I don't understand,' I said as I wanted to know how this miracle had happened.

'You boosted my confidence and that helped me during the interview,' he replied.

'Oh…it's OK,' I said.

It was another shock for me. It's very hard to digest one's own failure, but it's impossible to digest another's success. It's strange how quickly the tables had turned.

Courtesy wise I had to congratulate him so I did.

'Hey brother, congratulations, you deserve it,' I said.

'Thanks brother, but what about you?' he asked.

There was a sudden change in his tone. Just moments ago he'd been sounding like a deer trapped in front of a lion and now he was as bold as one.

'Well, it was not my day,' I responded diplomatically to hide my failure.

'Oh sorry, but you can crack any interview any day for sure,' he consoled.

'I know,' I smiled.

We parted for our respective destinations. I decided to walk rather than take a bus as I had ample time to kill. I attributed my overconfidence for my failure. It was tough to digest my first failure, but then nothing could be done. I mourned the failure of the interview for the next two days. However, to succeed one has to leave the past disappointments and concentrate on the future. Though I didn't want to go for any interview other than in Rohit's company he convinced me to give it another try. The interview in Rohit's company was scheduled for the coming week and I still had five days in hand, so I decided to give it another try.

For the next few days I kept myself busy getting interviewed but somehow I was getting rejected everywhere either because of my MTI (Mother Tongue Influence) or lack of prior experience. It kept on adding to my frustration. I was not sure what was happening with me. But I was not losing any sleep despite these failures as there was one last hope left for me—and that was in Rohit's company.

Interview II:
Rohit's Company

Finally the D-day arrived. Even though I had already faced failures in all of my previous attempts but this time I was quite sure about clearing the all-important interview. I had some reasons to support this. First, the interview was for a back-end process so stress would not be on paragraph reading (hopefully!). Second, Rohit's room partner was also working in the organization as an assistant manager and he assured me of getting employment. He assured me that one of his acquaintances would be conducting my final interview.

The BPO was located in NOIDA and as per Rohit it was one of the most reputed BPOs in India. It was a five-storied building with the company's logo Brilliance emblazon on it. One thing that amused me was the way they chose people to frisk at the entrance gate. The guard would ask you to select a ball from a covered opaque box and if you selected a coloured ball then you had to go through the frisking, otherwise if the colour of the ball was white then you could enter the premises without any probing even if you were carrying a live bomb. The process could be termed bizarre, yet I liked it.

However, here too the same procedures were followed regarding form filling and waiting for one's turn, the only difference being that the interviews were being conducted in the BPO premises itself rather than at a consultancy. For the first round which was a typing test, I was called in with five other candidates.

Though I was pretty comfortable with typing courtesy Internet chatting especially sex chats, but the test was a bit difficult as one needed to key in Russian words rather than only English words. I was sure I wouldn't be typing such words ever again in my whole life. To clear it one had to get at least 30 words per minute with at least 95 per cent accuracy. As soon as I took my seat, I started typing cautiously looking at each word and also keeping track of the time.

For the first time it seemed that all the money spent on Internet chatting wasn't a waste. I cleared the typing test without much difficulty. My typing speed was 35 words per minutes with 98 per cent accuracy. It was my first taste of success in the last one month so tears were about to roll down my cheeks. It was an emotional moment for me when the result was declared. I felt like a 4-year-old kid who had somehow survived the first day at play school without much trouble.

However, it seemed that only three out of five candidates could clear the typing test. As soon as I returned to my seat

I was handed a 30-page questionnaire. It had four sections, consisting of English Grammar, Mathematics, Analytical and Computer related general questions. I was asked to finish the paper in half an hour and hand it over to the HR rep. It didn't take long for me. Even a 9th-grade student could easily have answered them. I strongly believe it was high time for them to raise the standards.

The results were soon out and as expected I passed with flying colours, scoring 99 per cent. Again, tears almost started to roll out of my eyes. It was the first time in my entire academic career that I'd scored 99 per cent marks. I wish I could've scored even half that in my CA exams, then my life would have been more content.

Suddenly a middle-aged lady announced my name.

'Who is Shiv, please come forward.'

I raised my hand and followed her to her desk.

'Hi Shiv, I am Renu, from HR team in Brilliance. I just need a few details before I can send you for the final interview,' she explained.

As I'd already been assured by Rohit's room partner regarding the final interview, I was pretty assured that that day I'd come out of the building with an appointment letter in my hand. She asked questions related to my past experience, salary expectations, etc.

After that she completed my application sheet and asked me to wait in the lobby for my final hurdle.

I was soon called in by a person who would be taking my final interview, or say formal interview. He asked me to take my seat as we reached a small cabin.

'Hi, I am Sharmendra. I am recruiting for my billing process. Be comfortable and don't be nervous, take it easy,' he introduced himself. He was 5'5" tall, dark and heavy built. His one eye was squint.

He started the interview with general information like background, educational qualifications, etc. While I was answering he suddenly interrupted me and asked, 'OK Shiv, what is the root of 29?'

I was a bit flabbergasted by the sudden change of tack but didn't lose my concentration. I started doing a mental calculation. As I was busy calculating, I noticed the grin on his face.

'It's...741,' I answered hesitantly.

'Are you sure?' he asked cynically as he raised his left eyebrow.

I became doubtful so I started recalculating, soon realizing my blunder.

'Sorry, it's not 741, it's 841,' I replied apologetically.

'Don't worry, your answer is correct. I was just trying to test your calculation power,' he replied with a disarming smile.

'OK Shiv, how do you know Rohit?' he enquired, noticing the referral name on the CV. It was mandatory for every candidate to write the name of the referral on the application form.

'Rohit is my childhood friend and I also know his ex-room partner Manish who is an assistant manager here; he is also like an elder brother to me,' emphasizing more on Rohit's ex-room partner.

'OK, so you know Manish as well. That's good. Anyway, Shiv it was nice talking to you. The HR team will get back to you about the final results. You may leave for the day now.'

'Is the interview over?' I asked.

'Yes, please contact Renu and she will guide you about the final results,' he said as exited.

I'd noticed a drastic change in his facial expression the moment I'd taken Manish's name. I didn't expect the interview to end abruptly like that. I was informed that the final results would be communicated within two days. Except the last part everything went according to plan to make me feel content.

'Had I done something wrong by emphasizing more on Manish?' I wondered while leaving the premises.

As nothing further could be done I had to wait for two days to get my dream call, but as it was destined that call never came. Soon, two days became five but nobody called. During that period I ensured that my cell phone was fully charged and I even took the phone to the washroom to ensure not missing even a single call. But that elusive call never came.

After a week, I came to know from Rohit that I was rejected because I tried to influence the interviewer by taking Manish's name. This was my feedback given to him. My Earth came crashing down as it was the first time that a jack had worked the other way. It was like I had scored a self-goal by taking Manish's name. I was back to square one. I really didn't know whom to blame, whether Rohit, Manish or my fucking destiny. I didn't know when the dark clouds would go away.

Interview III: Success

I was neck-deep in frustration and didn't know how to get myself out of it. There was only one hope left and that too had abandoned me. There were too many people to be blamed for this mess: myself, Rohit, Manish, luck, God, the list seemed endless.

I didn't know why but I felt like celebrating my failure so I decided to booze that night. When you are frustrated you tend to indulge in all kinds of absurd activities. I'd read somewhere that in situations like these alcohol acts as a soother. It helps one to forget all worries. I wasn't sure about the authenticity of the fact, but it was time to find out.

'Let's have a party tonight,' I announced dejectedly.

'What!' Rohit shouted.

'Are you all right? I mean…' he queried as if he was trying to clarify that celebrations were meant for successes and not for failures.

'Yes, my friend. I want to celebrate my best friend's assurance. I want to enjoy *your* Manish's assurance of getting the fucking job,' I replied sardonically.

Ironically now 'my Manish' had become 'your Manish'.

'I'm sorry, Shiv. I didn't know that…' he said apologetically.

Somewhere down I knew it was neither his nor Manish's fault. It was destiny. The job was not meant for me so I didn't get it.

Simple, yet too hard to digest.

Realizing my mistake I too apologized for being sarcastic as I didn't want to lose my best friend.

I had lost enough in terms of confidence in the past few days.

'I'm sorry too,' I replied meekly.

Rohit once again proved that he was a true friend in every sense as he hugged me and soon all the differences melted away. But we stuck to my plan to celebrate my fiasco that night. I was still relying on my father's mercy (salary) to sponsor my stay in Delhi, so we restricted our quota of booze to only one bottle, and that too a *paoowa* or quarter, just 250 ml of whisky.

The next day I woke up late, my head still spinning like anything. I knew since my first drink that alcohol was not my cup of tea, but I was so maddened with my failure that I insisted on it that night. There was no point crying over spilt milk now; it was time to search for a medicine to get rid of the headache.

'Rohit…Rohit. Where are you? Do you have Disprin or anything?' I screamed.

But I didn't hear anything.

'Now where the hell has he gone?' I wondered as I grudgingly forced myself to get out of bed and started searching for some medicine.

I saw a piece of paper stuck on fridge's door.

'I'll be back by 10 p.m. Disprin is in the medicine box kept in my cupboard in case you need it. J'

The message brought a beam on my face. Well, this is what you call a true friend, someone who knows you in and out.

'God bless the bastard,' I smiled as I walked across to the cupboard.

Soon I could feel the power of the Disprin as my pain started to fade.

With abundant time to slaughter I logged on to the Net, porn sites to be precise. But when things are not going your way even the hottest porn stars on Earth with all their seduction can't distract your mind from the real issue, which was 'Finding a Job' for myself at the earliest.

I decided to turn off the system and reflect on the limited options left to me. Somewhere I wanted to save myself from the shame of watching porn without having a job. I guess watching porn with a job in hand would have made me feel less guilty.

I didn't know what made me look in my Yahoo email inbox before switching off the Net. As I was going through it I saw an email from a job site.

'Opening for voice process in Delhi based BPO, Prior experience not required, Salary package up to 14K plus perks' was the subject of the email.

'Why not try for this job?' a voice echoed in my mind. I knew that voice. You can call this the positive side of my mind which always believed that I could do anything, including screwing five women at one time. I assume that's an effect of watching too much porn.

'Are you crazy? Here I am unable to clear even the first round and you want me to go for another humiliation?' I retorted.

This reply came the from real me who till now had faced only disappointments in real life.

'I understand, but at least you can give one last try,' the positive side tried to inspire me.

'But…' the real side of me tried to raise the inevitable doubt of failure.

'No ifs and buts. You *are* going for this interview and that's it,' the positive side screamed, cutting short the doubts raised by the real me.

'At the most what would happen? You would fail again but at least you'd have tried. Isn't that a good thing?' the positive side tried to motivate me.

But the irony in life is unless you are successful, nobody is interested in your number of tries, but I didn't want to argue further.

'OK, I'll go for it tomorrow,' I reluctantly decided.

For the first time in life I elected to go with the positive side of my mind for reasons known to God only.

The next day I reached the We Guest BPO's office on Mathura road sharp at 11 o'clock as stated in the email. I had to go through the same procedures of submitting my resume, introduction, typing and written test rounds. But there was one test which was unique and very innovative, where I had to listen to a conversation between two people with US accents and based on that I had to select the right option. Most of the other candidates were a bit nervous but I was confident of clearing this round. I had a strong reason behind my confidence and I still feel very proud of it. My home was among the first few homes in my city which got a cable connection in the early Nineties when the cable TV revolution had just started, and because of that I used to watch English channels a lot. I started like any other sex-obsessed schoolboy but later on started taking interest in English movies.

Slowly I started to understand the language pretty well. As expected, this test turned out to be a cakewalk for me. But I didn't rejoice because of my recent failures as there was one final hurdle, the interview with the manager left between me and my elusive job letter. Soon that moment arrived as I took my seat in front of my potential manager. He too was not more than 25 years. He was lanky like me but far better in the looks department. He had grown goite, the one Aamir khan's character sported in Dil Chahta Hai. I was sure he too was younger than me. I wish I could have turned the clock back a couple of years and joined any call centre, at least I would have been something by now. But the unforgiving reality was that here I was sitting as a fresher and being interviewed by another schoolboy.

'Hi, I am Rahul Sati. I work here as a hiring manager,' his glib introduction brought me back to the real world.

'He…hello Sir. My name is Shiv,' I replied timidly.

'Don't be nervous. I am not going to eat you. Just relax,' He tried to pacify me.

Maybe I was panicking because of never-ending letdowns recently.

'Sir…may I say something if you permit?' I requested.

Somehow I didn't want to beat around the bush and get rejected at the end so I decided to do something against the standard interview procedure in the professional world.

'Yes, you can,' came the firm reply.

'Sir, I am sorry you may not like this but the truth is that I seriously need this job. I had appeared for umpteen interviews in the last one month but failed to clear even one: either I didn't have prior experience or for some other stupid reasons. I know only one thing, that this is my last chance otherwise I have to return to my home town,' I blurted.

I could notice his facial expression remaining impassive. Maybe in his entire hiring career he had never faced a loser like me.

Without paying heed to his poker face I continued.

'I just need one chance from you to prove my skill. I know I will have to work on my accent, but I can assure you that I will never give you a single chance to crib.' I gasped for air as soon as I finished.

There was a pin-drop hush in the room. He didn't utter a single word for the next few minutes and kept staring at me. And then he broke the silence with his stern voice.

'OK! Let me see what I can do.' he replied and left the room. It seemed the interview had ended.

I thanked God at least he hadn't kicked me out of the room. Irrespective of the final result, one thing was sure, that this experience would remain with me forever.

After some anxious 20 minutes a lady from the HR team came to announce the names of the selected candidates.

I was pleading to God, my most practiced activity of the last one month.

'Please God, this time please get me selected: this is my last chance,' I prayed.

Suddenly, I heard the most sought-after word of my life at that moment:

'Shiv.'

'Is that real?' I thought.

'S…sorry, could you please repeat that?' I requested.

I wanted to be sure that she'd announced my name.

'Shiv,' she said looking amused.

'Th…thanks, ma'am,' I mumbled. I could feel a lump in my throat.

Finally, the dark clouds had parted and the sunlight fell on me for the first time in a month. In my entire lifespan hearing my name never felt so joyous.

In life, when you are vying for something and in spite of all your efforts it remains elusive, one tends to imagine that once you conquer it you would rejoice like anything, but when that moment of conquest actually arrives you don't know how to react. I felt like hugging her and planting a kiss on her thick lips for announcing my name, but the very thought of landing in jail for sexual harassment halted me.

Then I felt like imitating Michael Jackson's moon walk step as my accomplishment was no less than that, but remembered my dancing skills so I left that option too. I just wanted to scream my lungs out and declare my victory to the world, but because of so many people out there I couldn't do that so I decide to celebrate my accomplishment outside the premises later.

Within half an hour the appointment letter was handed over to me. The happiness I felt was beyond words. I knew that I had cleared only a BPO interview, and that too after pleading to someone who was even junior to me in age, but it felt as if I had cracked the IAS exam. It was because I tasted triumph after so many rebuffs.

Between all this I forgot to thank Rahul for giving me a once-in-a-lifetime opportunity. So I looked for my savior but it seemed he was not there.

'May I have a word with Rahul?' I enquired with the HR lady near the reception counter.

'Sorry. He just went for an important meeting with the centre director.'

'OK, I'll wait then,' I said.

'I'm afraid it would take some time to get over,' she replied, with a questioning look.

'Is there anything important to talk?' she queried.

'Nothing much. Just wanted to thank him for this job,' I answered.

'You are Shiv, right?'

'Yes,' I replied raising my eyebrows.

'I have been asked by Rahul to hand this over to you,' she said, handing over an envelope to me.

I was a bit flabbergasted by this as I unfolded the paper to check the message.

'I have never done anything like this for anyone in my professional career. To be honest I don't know why I did this, but you are the first and the last one. I am giving you this opportunity because somewhere I felt that you are an honest soul. I hope you would never let me down in this company. Welcome aboard J - Rahul'

Once again tears welled in my eyes as I kept fiddling with the paper. I didn't know why I was behaving like a female, almost crying. I kept my head low to ensure that she couldn't see my face, but I was sure she could hear my sobs. It was really embarrassing for me to behave like a year-old wailing kid but I couldn't control it.

Before she could utter a single word I left the room with my prized possessions, my appointment letter and the beautiful message by someone whom I had met for the first time in my life. In-between all this I forgot to rejoice over my victory outside as I'd decided earlier, but I never ever repented it.

I didn't know that it was just the beginning, that there was a whole lot waiting for me. From that day onwards I was a part of the exclusive industry known as BPO. My induction date mentioned on my appointment letter was Aug 21, 2008.

'Hello, Papa, Shiv this side,' I rang my Dad.

'Haan, bolo…' he responded in his customary strict tone.

'Today I got hired with We Guest, a BPO company. The salary would be 14K plus incentives. My joining date is 21st August 2008,' I said.

'…and I am really sorry for having been a problem child for you,' I said after a pause of a few seconds.

I didn't know why I said so.

For a moment he didn't utter a single word and then he said, 'Congratulations. You don't have to say sorry; I shouldn't have forced you to go for CA anyway. I just pray to God that you attain lots of success in your chosen field,' he replied, lowering his tone for the first time.

It really felt overwhelming. It seemed that this new phase of my life might bridge the gap between the two of us.

'Give the phone to Mummy. I want to give her the good news personally,' I demanded.

Induction Day

Soon, 21st August 2008, my induction day arrived. It was a bright sunny day with no traces of clouds. I was ecstatic thinking about the events which would take place during the day.

'Have you seen my Induction Card?' I screamed while searching for it on the shelf.

My problem in life—sorry, one of my endless problems in life—is that I never keep my stuff in place and am very casual with things. I have been warned umpteen times by my family that I should learn to keep my belongings but an ass will remain an ass.

I knew that someday I might face the consequences but today was not the right day as I was getting late. I really didn't want to be late on the very first day of my professional life.

'Here's your Induction Card. You may have forgotten that you gave it to me to keep safely,' Rohit smiled as he flung the card towards me.

'Thanks Buddy, you're the best!' I hugged him and left for office. At times I thought I wouldn't survive without him.

If everything happens as per plan then obviously it was not my life: there had to be some hitch. Due to heavy traffic I reached We Guest office late by more than half an hour. I showed my Induction Card and hurried straight towards the auditorium as indicated by the guard. I cussed myself for not leaving my room an hour earlier. The fact was that I was late so I had no idea what was going to happen next.

I could hear the noise coming out of the auditorium. I paused at the gate of the auditorium and looked towards the rooftop. Since childhood we were taught that God exists everywhere, but how ironic that we always pray looking towards the sky in times of difficulty and nowhere else.

'God, please, *please*…save me,' I pleaded as I clutched my hands together.

I took a deep breath and pushed the door and left everything on God to take care of.

It was dark inside the room and slides were being shown on the screen. Everybody inside the room got distracted as light came in when I entered the room.

Every head in the room turned towards me as if an alien or celebrity (depending on one's choice) had made an entry.

'Look guys, we have a visitor; lets welcome him,' the presenter said as she paused the slideshow.

Before I could understand anything everybody started clapping before I could elucidate the reason for my delay.

Trust me it was disconcerting.

'Please come here on the stage,' the presenter asked me.

The presenter was in her early thirties, medium built, boy-cut hair, light brown eyes. She had strawberry lipstick. I could see her lips shining in the light of the projector. She was wearing formal clothes and was looking great in that outfit.

'Ahh…I was on time but due to heavy traffic…' I tried to explain as I moved slowly towards the stage.

'Hey, that's fine. Hi, my name is Sushmita. I am part of the HR team in We Guest and in charge of the Induction Session for the new hires. It happens, but because you are late you will have to do something for all of us,' the lady presenter said with a naughty smile.

'Am I right, people?' Sushmita asked for an audience poll.

'Yes!' everybody shouted.

'Something? What does she mean by "something"? I'm not going to do any striptease here,' I thought.

'Let's make him dance,' said somebody from the audience.

'No, make him sing,' another retarded from the audience proposed.

I began to get jittery.

First, I didn't know anybody, and then either I had to sing or dance in front of them. I was an introvert since my school days and suffered dreadfully from stage fright. I felt like a mouse in a trap. Though it was dark inside I could still see that around 20 people were sitting there.

'What's your name?' Sushmita asked.

'Sh…Shiv,' I stammered.

'So what have you decided? Dance or sing?' she enquired raising an eyebrow.

It was like questioning a married guy to make a choice between his mother-in-law and brother-in-law after 10 years of his marriage. Both these relationships are like pains in the ass. But given a choice the brother-in-law relationship is a better option to select for understandable reasons.

For me dancing was more a like mother-in-law so I elected to sing a song.

'I…I will sing,' I muttered.

'So everybody, please clap as he'll sing a song for us,' Sushmita announced as she clapped for me and others too joined.

Somehow I concentrated all my confidence and took the mike from her. As I opened my mouth to unleash my singing talent, somebody pushed the entrance door once again.

Everybody there got distracted once again.

For the moment I was calmed as somebody else had grabbed the momentum in the auditorium now. Instantly I wiped the sweat off my forehead.

'Thank God for saving my life,' I whispered.

'It seems that now you have company,' Sushmita said.

I was pleased to know that I didn't need to sing alone as someone else was going to share the discomfiture with me. As the person walked towards the stage I could easily figure out that she was a female though her face was not clearly visible due to the dim light in the auditorium. I could see the projector's light being reflected off her rose earrings. She was soon standing next to me on the stage. Now I could see her clearly.

My first reaction was as if I had been struck by lightning. It was the most stunning face I had ever seen in my life. She was about 22–23 years, extremely fair, her brown hair fell limply on her shoulders, she had an oval face, high cheekbones, and big brown eyes. Her light blue eye shadow highlighted her exquisiteness. She had rich pouting lips with light pink lipstick. She was looking exceptionally cute, wearing a white printed V-neck kurti which showed her prominent collarbone. Her black trousers fitted her loosely around her toned legs. She was wearing a golden colored bracelet on her right arm. Girls especially pretty ones have the ability to make even an ordinary bracelet look extraordinary.

Even she was not prepared for this unwelcome situation which was evident by the way she was clutching her bag tightly. Just like her, her pink bag was also cute. Her apprehension was evident on her face.

She also tried her best to explain the reason for her late arrival but it fell on deaf ears.

'What's your name?' Sushmita enquired.

'I…I am Tamanna,' she replied with a smile.

'Tamanna, what a lovely name, just like her,' I thought.

'He is Shiv and he too was late so now both of you have to sing a song together,' Sushmita explained the reason for my standing there. I wished she could have used a better way of introducing me rather than 'he too was late'. After all your first impression is your lasting impression.

'Hi, I am Shiv,' I introduced myself as I moved my hand forward for formal handshake.

Even though I wanted to hug her, but embracing—and that too in your first professional meeting—strictly states that you are a 'despo'. I wanted to avoid that term for myself.

Guys generally don't want to miss even a single opportunity to get physical with the opposite sex even if it's a mere handshake.

'Hello, myself Tamanna,' she replied as she shook hands with me.

'Oh, God what a touch,' I thought.

It was a hair-raising experience for me. It felt as if I'd touched a newborn baby's skin, it was so soft and silky. I thanked my stars as I was the first one who had any kind of physical contact with her in this company, not taking the lady guard's frisking into account.

I was sure that my 'blessing in disguise' situation must have become a matter of jealousy for the majority of the men there.

Just a few minutes ago I was feeling edgy and suddenly everything had turned around. The boring dark auditorium had been transformed into a happening and lively nightclub. The rectangular-shaped projector had turned into a revolving disc light. Even Sushmita was not spared; I could visualize her as a DJ who was busy belting out the latest hits. Even all the attendees present in the auditorium looked like regular club goers in their funky attires. I was busy envisioning in my own world when suddenly a shrill voice brought me back to reality.

At times reality sucks.

'So guys, please start. We're waiting,' Sushmita said.

The problem was that we both had to decide on a particular song though I was more interested in singing a romantic number now.

Suddenly, I started believing that I could give Sonu Nigam a run for his money. It was a ridiculous thought but I couldn't help it.

'Which song should we sing?' I asked her.

'Sing some brother-sister song,' somebody yelled from the crowd.

Everybody burst into laughter.

I was sure that guy didn't like me standing there with her. But the situation didn't allow me to respond so I just grinned even though I was totally pissed off by his comments.

Without delaying she settled on the song 'My Love' by West Life. No prizes for guessing her voice was as melodious as her beauty while mine was as terrible as me. I decided to act as a chorus and let her complete the song. There was another secret to my keeping mum: I hardly listen to English songs though I'd heard the band's name but that's the end of the story for me. I didn't want to ruin my reputation by saying no to her. While she was singing I just stood there and kept watching her, she was looking so cute.

I didn't know when the song ended as I was totally engrossed in watching her. I could only hear the applause. We were then asked to take our seats.

As I moved towards an empty chair, I prayed again, 'God, please, let her sit beside me.'

Luckily there was a vacant seat next to me and she did take it. I was on cloud nine again. I'd gone to cloud nine twice in past the 15 minutes. It seemed that everything started going in my favour the moment she entered the auditorium.

Then we got down to business. Sushmita gave us an overview of the organization as to when it was set up. I'm not sure whether it would ever become part of the history curriculum of any education board. Then she introduced the top-level management of the company. The business portrait of the CEO of the company showed him in a suit, shirt and matching tie, clean shaven and hair combed neatly backwards. However, his smile seemed to be a forced one. She moved from one slide to another at such a slow pace that could even make a tortoise feel like Michael Schumacher. I can define it in one word: mind-numbing.

I wasn't sure why she was keen to stuff us with so much information; it felt like the company hired her especially to brag about its superfluous junk. It was so boring that I almost slept there with my eyes open.

To get rid of boredom I decided to concentrate on Tamanna, the prettiest girl seated next to me.

I believe it was love at first sight or maybe it was infatuation. Though I was not sure about the emotion, but I didn't look at her chest even once. Normally this was not the case with other girls so I guess my feeling was more of love than of infatuation.

I was expecting her to start the conversation but somehow it seemed she was more interested in the boring slides.

Without wasting any more time, I started the conversation.

'Isn't it boring?' I asked her.

'Yes, but we can't do anything, can we?' she questioned.

I liked the way she responded.

'We have an option: we may go outside, else we may ask her to stop,' I proposed.

'Very funny,' she replied with a straight face.

My effort of trying to be extra smart fell straight on my face by her reply.

'Oh no, what have I done? I should refrain from acting too smart at the beginning. What impression I must have left on her,' I cussed my over-the-top sense of humour.

Rather than continuing the chat, I decided to concentrate (sleep) on the slides. Within five minutes I noticed that she kept looking at her cell phone. May be she was expecting somebody's call.

'Oh no, maybe her boyfriend. Why not? She's cute, she must have one. In today's world you'd hardly find a girl without a boyfriend, and if you're pretty then it's next to impossible.' My heart suddenly started beating fast. My love story ended even before it started

I thought I should clear this out straight. If she had a boyfriend then there was no point wasting time on her.

I gathered all my courage and asked the most frightful question a guy can ever ask a girl.

'Expecting a call?' Boyfriend? (mute)

The answer I was expecting from her was, 'No.'

'No, nothing like that,' she replied as she neatly slided her cell phone inside her purse.

'No, actually I noticed that your whole concentration was on your cell phone so I thought so. Sorry if you felt bad,' I clarified.

'That's OK, Sorry for my earlier comment.' Surprisingly, she apologized.

'Oh, no problem. It happens,' I made her comfortable as if nothing had happened even though I hadn't liked her reply then.

I was looking for such an opportunity to restart the conversation.

'So, is this your first job?' I asked her.

'No, my second,' she replied with a smile, a really pleasant one as I could see her pearl-shaped teeth.

'So it means you've been already through this torture,' I asked, pointing to the slides.

'Yes,' she chuckled.

'I love that smile,' I thought.

'Hey, control your emotions otherwise instead of an appointment letter they'll hand us a termination letter,' I advised her.

She laughed again. We do believe that if you were able to make a girl laugh there was some scope for you.

Suddenly, the lights were turned on and Sushmita announced.

'Take half an hour's break. Snacks have been arranged for you people outside'

Its corporate way of pampering before tying you to a slaughter machine.

'Would you like to come outside or should I get something for you,' I asked her.

'What can you get for me?' she asked fluttering her eyelids.

I was amazed by her response as I was least expecting that. I avoided direct eye contact as her misty eyes were making me weak.

However, I was ready with my typical roadside Romeo comment but with something added.

'I can get anything like the moon, or the stars, but right now only coffee or tea is on offer,' I replied.

'No, thanks, I'm okay,' she replied, giggling.

I left the room and headed for the break area. I was happy but at the same time suspicious regarding the call. Whose call was she expecting? Boyfriend? She didn't want to tell me so early or was just hiding it. Anyways, with all those questions arising in my mind I reached the coffee vending machine. There was a long queue so I just waited for my turn.

There was a girl in the queue right before me, I couldn't see her face, but it seemed she was not present in the audience. I probably missed her. Anyways when Tamanna was beside me it was very hard to look at other girls. Soon she pressed the button for tea, but I noticed she was having some problem with the machine. She was trying her best to get the coffee but somehow the machine was not responding. So I offered to help without even looking at her.

'May I help you?' I asked.

'No, I don't need help,' she replied rudely even without looking at me.

'How rude she is! No manners on how to talk to others especially to someone who was offering to help. Fuck off,' I thought.

She filled her cup and turned towards me. Her eyes were as expressionless as her response. She was about 5 feet 2 inches, with a fair complexion, big eyes, round cheeks as if she had '*rasgullas*' in each side of her mouth. She was of medium build, healthy but not fat. The best part of her feature was her hair. She had really long hair which went up to her waist.

I was least interested in her after the way she responded just moments ago so I simply got my cup of coffee and left

'Hi, Shiv,' somebody called my name as I turned my head towards the direction of the sound.

This guy had a heavy build, short crew-cut hair, a dark complexion, was clad in a T-shirt and jeans with a broad smile on his face.

'Hi…?' I replied trying to recognize his face.

'Prashant, you can call me Prat,' he introduced himself.

'Nice to meet you,' I replied

Soon we were chit-chatting with each other. Within a few minutes I came to know that he joined We Guest just to have fun, no serious stuff. He was waiting for his final year results and then would opt for an MBA course. Soon, the break ended and we returned to our seats. While entering the room I noticed Tamanna talking to somebody and looking a bit tense. I wasn't sure whether it was a mere coincidence, but the moment she saw me she disconnected her call, or maybe the conversation ended. I didn't want her to feel awkward so I behaved as if nothing had happened. However, the truth was that I didn't want to get a heart attack if she was talking to her boyfriend.

Soon we were handed over tons of forms to fill in the personal details.

'Do we need to fill all of them?' I asked Tamanna.

'Yes, all of them,' she grinned.

Anyways the day passed by filling up forms, I mean tons of forms. It was the only day in my life when I wrote my address more than 10 times. It made me remember our childhood punishment where we need to write a particular sentence again and again in school. I never wrote my address so many times ever in life. Though I know how to fill them but I purposely disturbed Tamanna for help.

We got our office access card, instant bank debit card, etc. My employee ID was 108. I didn't know when the day ended. Maybe it was all because of being in the company of a beautiful girl like Tamanna. While waiting for the cab I wanted to ask Tamanna's mobile number but didn't know how to approach her. Our next meeting would be only after three days.

Rather asking her directly I tried to employ my unused brain.

'Where do you live?' I asked her.

'Malviya Nagar, and you?' she replied.

'I stay in East Delhi, Shakarpur,' I replied.

'So, we'll meet on Wednesday,' I said in a gloomy manner.

'Yes, I know,' she agreed.

'So, may I have your number if you don't have any problem,' I asked hesitantly. I was worried about her reaction.

'Sure, it's OK. My number is 99104…..,' she replied casually. It's only with guys who give undue importance to stuff like this; for girls it's just a routine thing.

Now officially we had become friends. We both got our cabs and left for the day. It was a tiring day for me, a day when I met three of the most important people who would influence the course of my journey both professionally and personally (prospective life partner) in the coming days. I even started sending her SMS. I thought it would be better to start with SMS. Making calls so early may give a wrong signal to her which I really didn't want. I was quite happy with the new phase, I named it the 'One-sided love' phase. Though I had sent her more than ten SMS she didn't reply even once.

Training I: The Honeymoon Period Begins

24th August 2008 was my first day of voice and accent training. The shift timing allocated to me was 3 p.m. to 12 midnight. I was both exuberant and distraught at the same time. Exuberant because I would be learning a US accent, something total alien to me, and distraught because of Tamanna, who didn't reply even once. This was not expected from her, or maybe I had set high expectations from her a bit too early.

Thus, I decided that enough was enough and I wouldn't talk to her. I had to see my self-respect—male ego to be honest—and if I won't respect that then nobody else would. If she was showing attitude to me, I should also do the same. Courtesywise she should have replied at least once but she didn't.

I got ready on time and waited for the call from the We Guest transport team. Moments later my cellphone rang.

'Hello.' I said pressing the answering button.

'Is this Shiv?' The caller probed me.

'Yes. This is Shiv,' I answered.

'This is Manoj from the We Guest transport team. Kindly reach Aggarwal Sweets, your pick-up point. The cab will be there in 10 minutes,' he said.

'OK, I'll be there in five minutes,' I replied and hung up.

If someone has ever visited Shakarpur area in East Delhi, it's one of the most densely populated areas in Delhi. Buildings here look more like pigeonholes where you could stuff as many tenants as possible. The only objective of the landlords here is to earn as much as possible. As my room was located in the interior and due to traffic its narrow lanes become too congested I had mentioned Aggarwal Sweets as my pick and drop point to the transport team at We Guest.

However, I didn't know that this would create another problem, rather say a petrifying problem in the form of dogs chasing you at night during drop.

I reached my pick up point and waited for my cab.

I was excited to see my cab mates. Earlier I used to see others boarding BPO cabs and in almost all of them you would find pretty girls sitting. I had hardly seen a cab without a female so I was inquisitive to see my female cab mates.

In excitement I had almost emptied my new Axe deodorant bottle. After all your first impression is your lasting impression. I wanted to smell good.

But the cab didn't arrive. Soon 5 minutes became 10 minutes and then 15 but the cab didn't arrive.

I started thinking of all kinds of eerie reasons for the delay.

'Maybe the cab had moved off without me but I was on time and there is only one Aggarwal Sweets in this area,' I thought.

I was so engrossed in my thoughts that I forgot that I had the contact number of We Guest transport but soon better senses prevailed as I dialed them.

'Hi. Is this We Guest Transport?' I asked.

'Yes,' a male voice answered.

'I am Shiv. I am a new employee. My employee ID is 108. I was informed by the transport team half an hour ago to reach my pick up point Aggarwal Sweets. I am waiting here but the cab has not arrived.' I said in one breath.

'Shiv, one of the cab's tyres got punctured and the driver is changing it. It would take another five-ten minutes to reach your point,' he explained.

'Bastard, at least you should have informed me. I would have stayed back in my room. For the past half an hour I am baking my butt in 40 degrees,' I felt like yelling but somehow controlled myself.

'OK. I shall wait here,' I replied as I disconnected.

'God. Why do such things happen with me only?' I thought as I looked towards the sky looking for a response.

The heavenly response didn't come but my cab arrived after 10 minutes.

There was more discontent stored for me. There were only males in my cab. As usual my bad luck was running high. Now I was feeling bad for wasting my deodorant just to impress my own fraternity. I took my seat at the back. It took us half an hour to reach the office. Throughout the journey I kept on jolting my head either with the cab mate sitting next to me or with the top of the back door. It was a really irritating experience to sit at the back.

I rushed to the training room located in the basement. There were three training rooms adjacent to each other, each named after a flower. Our training was scheduled in Maple. For going to any of these rooms there was a passage running along them. There was one more room located at the end, a kind of recreational room where trainees could grab their cups of coffee and tea. It also had a bed to rest so at times it acted as a medical room too. For unknown reasons, there were not enough lights and being located at the end it resembled a haunted place more rather than a recreational room. Later I heard some rumours related to this room so I avoided going there alone.

I was concerned that training might have begun and I didn't want to get embarrassed by standing in the front once again. But this time I was more confident as I had a valid reason for my delay. But as I entered the room, there were hardly 10 people sitting there including the cutie girl Tamanna.

Even though I saw her flashing white teeth on seeing me through the corner of my eye, I simply ignored her and took my seat at the front.

'Hi, I'm Shiv. Has training not started yet?' I questioned the guy sitting next to me.

'Hello. No, not yet. The trainer's cab is late so class will start after half an hour. By the way my name is Hari,' he replied.

'Thank God. It's not only I whose cab was not on time,' I smiled as I shook hands with him.

'Where are the others? I hardly see anyone here. There were at least 20 people who joined with us but only half of them are present here,' I asked, my eyes roving around.

Once again I intentionally ignored looking directly at Tamanna.

'After it was announced that training would begin after half an hour most of them had left for coffee or a '*sutta*' break,' he replied.

'*Sutta* break?' I shrugged.

'*Sutta*' break means smoking break,' he grinned.

'Oh, actually I am new to this industry, so it'll take time for me to get used to the jargon,' I explained my helplessness.

As we were chatting I heard a lyrical voice calling out my name.

'Hi Shiv.' I knew the voice. It was Tamanna.

The moment I saw her cute face, I forgot everything including my self-respect philosophy; I forgot that she hadn't replied to any of my 10 SMS even though all of them were forwarded ones talking about friendship and life. Initially, I refrained from sending love SMS as that would give wrong signals. I just couldn't afford to lose a girl like her.

'Hi Tamanna,' I replied as I strolled towards her. I didn't even care to say the courtesy bye to Hari.

It was obvious that when a pretty female is calling out your name, you don't care about the world around you. Poor Hari was the part of that world.

I sat next to her.

'Are you upset with me?' she asked, blinking her eyes as if to complain that how could I ignore a pretty girl like her.

She was right. 'How stupid I could be. She has not done any crime by not replying to my stupid SMS but she did flash her million-dollar smile when I entered the room,' I thought, cussing my stupidity.

'No…it's just that I didn't notice you,' I tried desperately to control the damage.

'Oh OK. Then it's fine. I thought you were angry because I didn't reply to your SMS. I don't believe in sending forwarded SMS, it's so childish. When you have an option to talk then there is no point in sending SMS,' she justified for not replying.

She had a valid point. It's really childish behaviour to send forwarded SMS. But what did she mean by 'When there is an option to talk'?

'Does she want me to call her?' I thought.

This is one of the many divine powers which every female possesses, the power to puzzle men with their sugary words. No one except them will ever know the true sense of it.

While I was busy unraveling the real sense of her words even though I knew I would fail miserably, somebody patted on my back.

'Hi Shiv.' It was Prashant standing there.

'What a timing the idiot has,' I thought.

'Oh hi Prashant. How are you?' I asked reluctantly.

'Well, life is tough but it seems you are enjoying every moment of it,' he smirked.

I knew what he meant by 'enjoying every moment'. Before I could utter any further he said.

'Hey brother, whenever you're free let me know; I need to talk to you,' he said.

It seemed that everybody there wanted to talk to me. For the first time I felt as if my existence had some kind of importance in this world.

Even though I didn't want to introduce him to Tamanna but with no choice left I had to. Prashant was far better in the looks department and his lifestyle clearly suggested that he belonged to a financially sound family. In today's materialistic world it's like digging your own grave by introducing 'your girl' to someone who is better than you in every department. Though I would have loved to introduce him on *Rakhi* day.

'Tamanna, he's Prashant. Prashant, she's Tamanna (inaudibly) your sister-in-law,' I introduced them to each other.

Even though it was just a normal handshake between them but it felt like someone had jabbed a knife in my chest. It was only when their hands parted that I felt relieved.

As expected Prashant placed his butt on the seat next to mine. As I was about to resume my conversation with Tamanna someone walked hastily inside the room. Soon the other absentees from my batch followed suit.

'Hi everyone. First of all, sorry for being late as you can't control the traffic in Delhi,' he expressed his regret for being late.

'I understand,' I thought trying to sympathize with his situation.

'My name is Varun. I will be your voice and accent trainer for the next two weeks,' he introduced himself.

He was quite fair, tall, and average built. In short a good-looking guy. As usual he too appeared younger than me in age. Even though he was bald still he could give any guy with good looks tough competition. It would be a nightmare for me to even envisage myself without hair. Even a monkey without hair would look better.

However, I liked what he said at the end of his speech.

'I have one request to make. Please don't call me sir. Remember, this is not a school: we all are professionals here and anybody calling me sir would have to treat me.'

'OK Sir,' somebody from the crowd shouted.

Everybody present burst out in laughter.

'So we'll start with formal introductions. It would consist of your background, educational qualification and your professional experience if any,' he announced.

It was a real humiliation to introduce myself there. Among the batch of 20-odd joinees only one guy was older than me but had six years of prior work experience. I was really feeling ashamed sitting there, especially next to Tamanna. God knows what impression I left on her after all this.

Soon the trauma ended as we got our first break.

Training II: The Honeymoon Period Continues

'OK guys, listen. Here is your training plan. The voice and accent training will be conducted for two weeks and then there will be one week for process training,' Varun announced as he circulated the training plan in the training room.

My eyes ran through the words mentioned in the leaflet.

'What is this '*' mark for?' Prashant questioned.

'Good question,' Varun smiled.

'I hope others too have the same doubt.'

Everyone present in the room raised their hand in reply.

'Well, this asterisk means only if you are able to clear voice and accent assessment will you be eligible for process training,' he revealed the mystery behind the asterisk mark.

Some people started looking at each other's faces. There were a few including Tamanna who didn't look concerned with this new development at all as if to suggest this hurdle would be as small as the size of asterisk on this paper to overcome.

However, this new announcement brought sweat beads on a few foreheads including mine.

Somehow Tamanna understood my anxiety, and tried to soothe me.

'Don't worry. You would clear this hurdle,' she whispered as she touched my hand.

For the moment I forgot my concern regarding clearing the assessment and was back again to cloud nine flying with her. It felt so good.

Now I needed this job even more, not only for the money but for her too. I just couldn't let her go away.

'Thanks for the concern,' I said as I placed my other hand on top of her's. It felt like heaven.

'Don't worry guys. My track record is 100 per cent. Nobody has ever failed in my training,' Varun proclaimed.

Even though it sounded like bragging it did bring some respite to our faces.

'If you can make me cross this hurdle only then will I accept this as truth,' I challenged him mentally.

Somewhere down I knew that the coming two weeks would be one of the most challenging weeks for me in terms of my professional life.

Before I could recover from the first shock, another shock was waiting for me. Varun circulated another printout.

'Now what the hell is this for?' I thought.

'Guys, I would like each one of you to go through the paragraph one by one to evaluate your current level of speech. Based on your individual performance, the one with good accents would sit at the back and those with not so good ones would sit at the front,' he announced.

There was only one thing which was as per my wish and that was sitting next to Tamanna but it seemed that God didn't like that either. My stomach was churning due to nervousness.

One by one everybody started reading out their handout while I waited for my humiliation, sorry, turn. It was like a live bomb ticking that could explode any time. Eventually it did explode and the results were out. I never saw Varun writing so much on his sheet while I was delivering my speech. He looked worried once I finished my speech. He must be thinking that here was a guy who could break his 100 per cent record.

As expected I was asked to move my ass to the front row. Tamanna would remain seated at the back. Even Prashant did better than me so he was asked to sit behind me.

'Don't worry, it happens,' Tamanna tried her best to console me in the cafeteria where I was sitting with my head down and with a pout.

'Even I scored badly, Shiv but I'm happy,' Prashant babbled.

'I'm not here to have fun. This is serious business for me. After getting fucked up for two months I got this job and I just can't let it go,' I screamed as I banged my fist on the table.

I am not sure whether I had overreacted but I didn't like his carefree response. One needs to be serious at times.

'Just leave me alone,' I said as I stomped out of the cafeteria.

Both Tamanna and Prashant were stunned by this sudden outburst. They didn't expect me to behave like that.

Prashant didn't utter a word and moved out of the cafeteria for his smoke. Only Tamanna remained there sitting quietly all alone.

I went out and seated myself near the open space adjacent to the main building.

I was feeling dejected sitting there when somebody offered me a glass of water. As I looked back Tamanna was standing there with the water in her hand.

She didn't utter a word, just offered me the glass. Even I didn't look at her, just grabbed the glass and gulped it in one go. I needed it.

After a few minutes of silence, she finally spoke.

'Are you all right?'

'Yes…I'm fine,' I muttered.

Again she didn't speak for a few minutes. Maybe she was waiting for me to get back to normal.

'May I ask you something?' she enquired.

'Yes. Yes, you can,' I replied trying to hold back my tears.

'Whatever happened a few minutes back, was it your fault or somebody else's?' she asked.

'I guess…it was mine,' I replied sheepishly after a long pause.

'Then why did you scream at Prashant? He was just trying to calm you down,' she said.

I didn't reply.

'Now you have to apologize,' she murmured.

'No I won't,' I replied.

'Listen Shiv. This is not your school or college. This is a professional world where for a career growth your own teammates or so-called friends will scheme against you. In this world you never know when your friends will become your enemies. I am saying this because I have been through all this,' she said.

'You are lucky to have Prashant as your friend so early in your professional life. Try to respect this fact,' she continued.

'I don't care,' I replied firmly. Even though I cared for what she was speaking, it was my ego which was stopping me.

'OK then. We can't continue as friends now. One day you would behave with me also like this. I thought you to be different but you are also like others,' she said as she stood up.

Girls, especially pretty girls, know how to play with your emotions. Even though it was a kind of blackmail but they are convinced that this weapon won't go in vain.

So I surrendered. After all an apology would keep her in my vicinity.

'No...no. Please don't go. I'll apologize,' I pleaded.

'Let's go to the smoking area. He told me that he was going for a *sutta* break,' she smiled. Her smile depicted her victory once again.

I followed her half-heartedly towards the smoking zone.

I could see him blowing smoke rings out of his mouth. He seemed to be an experienced smoker. Now I was feeling guilty for being responsible for this particular smoke.

'Prashant. Please come here. Shiv wants to talk to you,' she called out.

'Coming,' he replied, throwing his half-burnt cigarette and walking towards us.

'Yes?' he asked.

I could see Tamanna popping out her eyes to signal that it was my turn to speak.

'I am…I am…' I mumbled with my head down.

'Shiv!' she scowled.

'I am sorry,' I muttered as fast as I could. To apologize is one of the toughest tasks in the world. It takes a lot of effort to say sorry. But somehow I conquered it and was feeling relieved.

'It's OK. It happens,' he replied.

All of a sudden he hugged me.

I didn't expect it, but Tamanna was right. He was a good guy. I too embraced him. Anyways you can't argue with females. There's only one set formula for them: either they are right, or you are wrong.

We three returned to our training room with smiles on our faces.

Training III:
The Honeymoon
Period is Over

It'd been a week since the training started but it felt like being married for 10 years. Our voice and accent training was going on in full swing and so was our friendship. Tamanna, Prashant and I had become good friends though at times Tamanna behaved like a stranger especially whenever she had to talk privately on her cell phone. I was sure that she had been talking to her boyfriend but was not sure why she was hiding it from me. At the same time I had no courage to ask her.

Varun was trying his level best to make us speak like an American but there were a few who were equally trying their best to prove him wrong and I was one of them.

Our daily routine included 'kissing our Ws, biting our Vs and rolling our Rs'. I am not sure when I last rolled my tongue so much. One thing was sure that I would soon end up in a dentist's cabin for jaw dislocation.

Apart from the three of us there were other characters too in our training room. There was this guy Ashok who was in his mid-thirties, heavy built and for some strange reasons he kept digging his nose in front of others. He resembled a grown-up chimpanzee and was a live example of the fact that monkeys were our ancestors. Everybody in our class refrained from shaking hands with him. But he possessed one good quality: his accent was the best among the guys.

Then there was Sanjay, around six feet tall, a dark-complexioned guy. He was always interested in sex-related chats. You would always find his eyes full of lust. Once he told us that he could arrange call girls for us. Not sure whether he was lying but he did show me some numbers in his cell phone.

There was another guy named Manish. Probably his height stopped the moment he passed Class Six. If someone met him for the first time he would definitely mistake him for a child. But he was extremely gregarious and it made him a favourite among the females.

Among the girls we had Deepika who always wore flat sandals because of her height. She was even taller than a few males in the class. She was fair and good looking but because she always behaved like a supercilious person, most of the people in the classroom avoided interacting with her. Once while having dinner in the cafeteria, I saw her soaking up the vegetable oil from the *puris* using tissue paper. It looked really weird. She always ate less as compared to her figure. Not sure whether she was on a diet or not. Maybe she gorged once she reached home. You never know but some females do that purposely.

And then we had Puja, famous for two reasons. One, for her curly 'Maggie' hair and secondly for her love of body-hugging clothes. Her assets looked too prominent in those dresses, but once Tamanna told me that she hardly cared. I was sure that she could be one of the reasons for Sanjay's lustful eyes. For others I could only say they were like unsung heroes of the class. In schools we used to have three types of students one who used to sit at the front and were brilliant in studies, second type of students who preferred to sit at the back and were always on the hit list of teachers for their naughtiness. But there was the third type of students who were the most neglected ones. These students were neither mischievous nor vivid. So apart from these characters I hardly got to know anyone else. But one thing was common among them: they all were performing better than me.

Even though I was trying my best to get promoted from the first row but there were others who were trying even better.

'I think I love her,' I said while peeing in the washroom.

'So what…?' Prashant replied nonchalantly.

Because he was busy drawing a masterpiece with his pee, he didn't pay attention to what I thought.

'I love her. Idiot!' I reiterated.

'So what's the problem?' he replied indifferently.

'I thought you would show some kind of emotions?' I asked.

'The way you stare her, the way you get tea, coffee for her, the way you search for her cab first before yours during drop, do I still need to show emotions?' he grinned.

I didn't utter a word. The bastard knew everything.

'But there is one problem,' I said.

'What?'

'I'm not sure whether she has a boyfriend or not,' I said, zipping up.

'I want to find out the truth and you need to help me out,' I said.

'But you can ask her directly.'

'I just can't. I even tried to ask her but the very thought of her having a boyfriend petrifies me. Try to understand my situation,' I said gloomily.

'It's only been a week, but it seems that I know her since ages. I have to stop myself before it's too late,' I continued.

'OK. No problem. I'll find out the reality for you,' he assured as he tried to embrace me.

'You ass! At least you should have washed your hand!' I yelled as I pushed him away. He burst into laughter.

Later that night we three were having dinner in the cafeteria. That night's special menu was Egg Day. However, there was a placard placed in front which clearly stated that Only One Egg per person. I was OK with it but not sure about the others. Prashant was pissed off with the instructions.

'Have you seen the size of the egg?' Prashant asked furiously.

'What's wrong with it? It's only small in size,' I replied as I stirred the egg to look for any other flaw.

'Small? I don't think so. These are underdeveloped eggs. Not sure from where they've got these so-called eggs,' he was really agitated. 'It seems they forced the hens to produce eggs.' The way he said it brought smiles to our faces.

It was only when I offered my egg to him that he calmed down.

'Hey guys. I have interesting news for you all!' Tamanna said excitedly.

'What?' I said as I stopped eating but it had no effect on Prashant. He continued nursing his appetite.

'Varun would be taking us to the operation floor for live barging-in. Isn't it exciting?' She replied.

'Yes. I hope so,' I sighed.

I had never ever visited any calling operation floor but with God's grace it would soon become my second home.

The next day we all got our first opportunity to see what it actually felt like being on a call.

It was a huge hall divided into cubical bays. Each U-shaped bay had five workstations on each side. There must have been at least 15–20 cubicle bays like this in the entire hall. Midway they had the most dreadful workstation known as 'traffic'. Dreadful because this system would show whether you were on 'Ready Status' or not, and whether you were deliberately avoiding incoming calls. And God forbid if you tried any of those tricks there would be someone who'd be shouting his lungs out to make you answer the call. That's why this person was referred to commonly as '*Yamraaj*, the God of death' of the calling world.

Because of the calling, I thought that there would be pin drop silence on the floor but the moment I entered the floor it resembled a fish market more. I could hear people bawling. There were a few who were standing and taking calls. The atmosphere was of sheer pandemonium.

I wondered how one could even think of taking calls in such a messy environment. Soon Varun asked each one of us to sit next to a live caller. I was escorted to the first bay along with Sanjay. Tamanna moved to the third bay while Prashant moved even further to tenth bay or so.

At first I didn't notice that I was seated beside a female caller. I was more worried about Tamanna being seated beside a male caller.

I couldn't see her face as she was totally engrossed in her call. She was clutching her headset with both hands and trying to make sense of what the other person was speaking on the other side.

We parked our butts on the seats placed next to her.

'Once she finishes with this call, she'll make you listen to the next call,' Varun informed us and moved to the other bay.

I could see a filthy smile appearing on Sanjay's face. His eyes were getting lustier with each passing moment.

'What?' I animatedly asked him.

He didn't utter a word. He just moved his eyes towards the female caller.

My eyes followed his as I was curious to know the reason for his smutty smile. As I turned towards her I got my answer. As she was leaning on her desk, her bare essentials were getting exposed.

'Fuck you,' I muttered animatedly to him. He just sniggered.

There was no point trying to straighten a dog's twisted tail so I started looking at my surroundings. It's all too easy to differentiate between a male's desk and that of a female. You'd find countless short messages pinned on her wall. Even though she'd have spent several years in the company, you'd still find messages from her first year pinned around her desk. The similarities between all the messages would be about people talking about how beautiful her smile was and so on. You'd also find some small ugly fur toys placed near around workstation. To complete the setting you could also see some luminous stickers mostly of butterflies pasted on the walls of the monitors.

Only God could tell about their fascination for butterfly stickers.

As for men, you'd hardly find anything pinned on the wall other than work-related boring stuff. Boring!

Somehow I felt, looking at her, that I had seen her somewhere, however, not sure when and where.

As I was trying to recall, her call got over and she turned towards us.

'Hi guys. My name is Radhika and I will be mentoring you both,' she introduced herself.

As soon as she turned towards me, I recognized her. She was the girl who behaved rudely with me at the coffee machine on my induction day.

'Come on, God. Out of some hundred-odd callers you found her for me. Not fair,' I thought.

But as instructed by Varun she would be mentoring us. Nothing could be done now.

'Hi, I am Sanjay and he is Shiv,' Sanjay introduced us. He even shook hands with her. Now I was feeling pity for her because of Sanjay's prying eyes. It seemed that even she didn't notice me. OK, I accept I was not Hrithik Roshan, but she should have remembered that she misbehaved with me.

'Hello,' I replied half-heartedly and made sure not to shake hands with her.

Before we could continue with our chat, her phone beeped.

'Hey Shiv, pick the adjacent receiver and listen to the call,' she instructed me as she pressed the answering button.

I followed her instructions obediently.

'Hi, my name is Alias. How may I help you?' she introduced herself pleasantly.

For your information Alias was her pseudo name so that the Americans couldn't recognize that their calls were being attended by an Indian.

'Hello Alias. This is Andrew. How are you and how's the weather there?' The caller asked.

I was thrilled to hear a live American voice. Surprisingly, the best part of the call was that I could hear it clearly and was able to comprehend what he was looking for.

'I am doing fine and the weather here is pleasant. Thanks for asking,' she replied.

'Well I want to update my address,' he stated.

'Sure. I would be glad to assist you,' she said cheerfully.

'In order to update your address, I need to verify your SSN and your current address,' she continued.

'I'm ready with my details. Let me know when to start,' the customer answered.

'You seem pretty much aware of the process,' she acknowledged the customer's awareness.

I liked the way she was building a rapport with the customer.

Soon, as a seasoned executive she provided the resolution and wrapped up the call. It was a perfect call as per my understanding. I was impressed by her call handling skills.

She put herself on 'Not Ready Status' to discuss the call with me.

'So did you like it?' she asked.

'The call was good but I didn't like your behaviour then,' I thought.

'The call was really good,' I eventually replied.

'So can any one of you tell me what the customer was looking for?' she questioned spreading both her palms.

Even though Sanjay too had listened to the call but his main area of focus was more on her physical appearance than on listening so he was clueless.

'I think the customer was looking for his address change?' I said.

'Bull's eye!' she said ecstatically, approving my response.

'You know Shiv, when I did my first barge-in I couldn't understand a word but you did it. That's commendable,' she smiled.

Her words of admiration acted as a catalyst as I became more confident.

We spent almost an hour with Radhika and she handled each call like a perfectionist. My bitterness towards her was getting lesser with each passing call.

After Some Time: In the Cafe

'So how was your experience?' Tamanna enquired blinking her eyes as usual. I still don't know whether she did that intentionally or not.

'It was really good. My mentor Radhika was too good. The whole experience boosted my confidence. It'll surely help me in my final assessment,' I said

You can only expect a female to make something out of nothing. Calling Radhika my mentor and praising her made Tamanna's facial expression change from happy go lucky to an agitated 'How dare you' one. The damage had been done and it was time to face the consequences.

I could see Tamanna getting hyper. I had noticed that whenever she got hyper she starts gyrating few of her hairs around her nose. I know it's outlandish behaviour but when you consider it's by a female you would consider it as normal.

'But you know, Prashant, I have never heard a better caller than Tamanna,' I tried to control the situation.

'By the way when have you heard her calls?' he questioned me mischievously.

'I...I mean not her call but her speech during the training. Everyone including Varun clapped for her on our first day of training,' I said wiping sweat beads from my forehead.

'Oh OK,' he replied.

'Bastard!' I scowled.

Suddenly an idea came, '...and you know, Tamanna, she was the one who behaved rudely with me on the induction day. You *remember* I did talk to you about it,' I said emphasizing the word remember.

'Really?' she replied, trying to recall. I clearly remembered that I did talk to her about the incident and how annoyed I was then. I was just hoping she recollected all that.

After two minutes of absolute silence she spoke up, 'Oh yes. I do remember that.' I could see her facial expressions getting back to normal.

'Thank God,' I whispered.

'Even though she's a good caller I didn't like her behaviour,' I added.

It further mollified her and I liked that.

'OOOOuch,' I bellowed.

'What happened?' Tamanna enquired.

'N…nothing,' I replied. Prashant tapped my toe on seeing me escaping unhurt.

'Fuck you,' I muttered, looking at him. I was relieved to survive this catastrophe. I'd learnt my lesson to never laud a female to another female. You may not be lucky enough to escape unhurt every time.

Judgement Day

'Guys, calm down. It's just an assessment and not a life and death situation,' Varun was addressing our batch just before the commencement of our final assessment.

'It's a life and death situation for me at least,' I thought.

He was trying his best to boost our confidence so that his 100 per cent track record remained intact. However, the facial expressions of quite a few including me in the training room were like appearing for their Class 10 Board exams once again. It was a dreadful experience then. Trust me nobody in the world wants to revisit those moments ever especially the first day of the Board exams.

'Remember what I told you. Patience is the key to success here. Listen carefully what the request is for and then provide the resolution. Believe me nobody on Earth can stop you from succeeding,' he continued.

'So once again best of luck guys,' he concluded his motivational speech.

The judgment day had finally arrived. Before dusk I would get to know whether I could continue with my side of the love story with Tamanna or not. I had decided that if I failed to cross the hurdle, I would never talk to her. The very thought of not seeing her cute face was making me panicky.

'Shiv, don't worry. Everything will be all right,' Tamanna tried to comfort me.

'And if not?' I asked.

'Don't be so negative in life. Haven't you heard what Varun said just few minutes back?' she replied.

'What?' I asked absent-mindedly.

'That you just need to listen carefully and everything will fall in place, idiot,' she almost screamed.

'Oh yes, I do remember that,' I replied, my head down. I was still engrossed in my thoughts.

'Shiv, just look at me,' she implored. Immediately I turned my face towards her.

'Just follow that,' she smiled.

'Will do,' I replied, smiling back at her.

'She really cares a lot for me,' I thought.

Prashant had already started his assessment. I was sure he would come out smiling. There was no doubt about Tamanna clearing the assessment. Doubting Tamanna's capability to overcome this hurdle was like questioning Sachin Tendulkar's ability to score runs. So the only person left was me.

I was soon asked to go into a quiet room with a setting similar to that of the operation floor. I was informed that my process manager would be taking my assessment. I would be marked on two parameters: one would be voice and accent, and the second process knowledge.

I wore my headset and waited for my call. My heart was beating faster than the engine of a superfast train.

'Don't get nervous. Don't get nervous,' the thought echoed in my mind.

Soon my Avaya phone beeped. I took a deep breath and pressed the answering button.

'Thank you for calling Finger Home. My name is Shiv... sorry, Scott. How may I help you?' I recited my introductory line.

'Is it Shiv or Scott?' The caller enquired.

'Shit' (silently). It's Scott,' I replied.

'OK Scott. I am looking for the balance amount in my account. Could you help me?' the caller asked.

'Sure Sir. May I have your first and last names?' I enquired.

'My name is Dinah Moore,' he replied.

'OK, thank you. Please give me a moment while I check the balance amount,' I replied.

'Sure,' he said.

I placed the call on mute and started turning the pages of my notebook. But as expected I didn't find the procedure written there. It didn't take long for me to realize that I had brought the wrong notebook.

'Fuck you,' I thought. Lines appeared on my forehead. I couldn't believe that I had dug my own grave. Tears rolled out of my eyes.

'You there?' I could hear the customer enquiring at the other end.

'Yes...I'm here,' I replied hesitantly.

'I would request you to give me some more time to look for the information,' I said.

'OK. Take your time,' Dinah replied.

I could imagine myself waving good bye to Tamanna and Prashant. I couldn't even blame anybody else. It was my mistake and I had to bear the brunt of it. With no other options and only two minutes left before I would eventually flunk, I closed my eyes. Tears kept on rolling out of my eyes.

Suddenly Varun's words started echoing in my mind.

'Patience is the key here. Don't panic. Just listen carefully and then answer.'

Even Tamanna asked me not to overlook this.

Realizing that, I wiped my tears and soothed myself. I recalled the process flow on how to handle the account balance. Within a few seconds I could see bulb lighting in my mind, in short I got the answer.

'If he is looking for his balance, he should provide me his SSN number,' I thought.

I hurriedly unmuted the button.

'Sorry for being on hold. I apologize for the inconvenience. In order to assist you with your account balance I would need your SSN number,' I said.

'You need what? SSN?' He asked.

'Yes Sir, we need that,' I replied.

I was pleading to God that he falter in providing his SSN number as I was not sure of the next steps. There is this saying that there is a time in a day when your prayers are acknowledged by the Almighty. For me this was that time.

'I am sorry but I don't want to share my SSN,' he replied.

'I apologize, but without the SSN, I won't be able to provide you the details,' I said cheerily.

Even though I had to empathize with the customer, I was elated by his response.

'Can't you provide the details without the SSN? It's important,' he said.

'I really apologize Sir, without the SSN details we won't be able to provide you the balance amount. It's to safeguard your account,' I replied.

'OK. Thanks,' he said.

'Thanks for calling Finger Home. Have a great day,' I concluded the call.

I was relieved. I still couldn't believe that I had finally been able to overcome this impediment.

Soon the results were out and as expected Varun's 100 per cent record remained intact. One should have seen the smile on his face. He was more relieved than anybody else in the training room.

'I am so happy for you,' Tamanna congratulated me.

'Th…thank…you,' I stammered. She chuckled.

Before we could continue with our conversation, Prashant rushed from the other end of the room and lifted me.

'I knew it, I knew you'd crack it!' he almost screamed.

'Thanks. Thanks a lot, dear,' I replied as I too hugged him.

From then onwards I was on the payroll of We Guest and had a confirmed job.

I wanted to take my friendship with Tamanna to the next level but somehow didn't feel it was the right time to speak so I postponed it for some other time. We all were busy congratulating each other on the triumph.

Now we all were ready to take plunge in the real world of calling.

Go-Live Day

It had been more than three weeks since I had joined We Guest but salary eligibility wise, it was my first day in the office. Going forward, I would be getting paid for every second spent in the company. Even though we all had cleared the mock calls but we still had to face the real challenge that was handling live calls. As they say, facing real life is altogether a different ball game.

As instructed a day before, the entire training batch was supposed to meet in the training room for one last time and from there we were supposed to go to our respective bays.

I reached there on time courtesy the early arrival of my cab. However, sitting in the back seat of the cab was still a pain for me. Usually my pick was the last pick on the route so I had no option than to sit at the back. For unknown reasons the middle row was always booked for females. It was like an unpublished law in We Guest that all men had to follow. I wished that someday it would get changed. Earlier

I was in an all-men cab so I had some rare opportunities to sit in the front but for the past one week I had been moved to a co-ed cab. Now I hated it even more not only because I had to sit at the back but also none of the female cab mates were even worth mentioning.

Prashant had already reached before me. Tamanna's cab was late so it took another 15–20 minutes for her to reach office.

'Hi brother,' he greeted.

"Hello Prashant. How are you?' I responded.

'Well, not so good,' he said. I'd hardly ever seen him in low spirits so there was something wrong.

'What happened? Why you are sounding so low?' I enquired.

'Nothing. Just feeling nostalgic about this training room. We spent so much time having fun here but moving on it would be just calls and calls. There is a strong possibility that we might have different shifts and we may not get time to even meet each other,' he murmured.

'I know,' I replied.

'So going for dinner or on breaks together would become a rarity for us in the near future,' he continued.

'My dear, I completely agree with you but unfortunately this is professional life and we all were hired to take calls so we need to adhere to the company's policies. As for not spending time together we may request our supervisor to align the three of us in the same shift or shifts close to each other's. This way we shall remain in touch,' I tried to lift his spirits.

'We shall remain in touch with each other. If by chance we are unable to meet each other in office we have the option to meet outside on weekends,' I said.

It brought relief visible on his face as the tense lines on his forehead evaporated. Even I was worried about the same thing but somewhere knew that we couldn't do much about it. Soon we were joined by Tamanna. Even she didn't look too pleased about leaving the 'honeymoon period'. Perhaps this was the first and the only time when I was soothing both of them rather than them soothing me. The feeling was great.

As we were yakking, Varun made his entry.

'So guys how are you?' he shouted.

'Good!' everyone present shouted.

'Are you ready to go live?' he asked.

'Yes we are,' everybody present there yelled again.

'Good!' he replied.

'Before we disperse I just want you people to know that you were the best batch I ever got to train, so thanks for being so kind to me. Though my training has ended but I would still be there for all kinds of succor. You all have my number so feel free to contact me. Best of luck for your future and make yourself proud,' he concluded his touching farewell speech.

I could see drops falling from her eyes. I didn't utter a single word, but just offered my hanky, making sure that it was clean. Just looking at her made me feel like crying but somehow I controlled my emotions. Soon everyone started embracing and wishing luck to each other. I could see a few people making the most of this opportunity. Ashok, the nose digger was able to shake hands with each one of us for the first time. However, I could see a few people running towards the restroom after the handshake. Even Deepika had toned down her behaviour and was surprisingly, acting like a normal girl. It was both emotional and hilarious at the same time.

As communicated earlier, each one of the new associates would be sitting next to their mentors so that in case of any problem they could dig us out of it. I was seated in the first bay, Tamanna moved to the third bay, and Prashant was seated at the last. The seating arrangement was similar to the mock call session. For reasons unknown Sanjay was asked to sit beside a male caller. It was a last-minute change; probably Radhika had anticipated his filthy intentions.

'Hi Radhika!' I greeted my mentor as I moved into the first bay where she was seated.

'Hi Sh…Shiv, right?' She questioned pointing her finger at me.

'Right,' I grinned.

'Here's your system. Login with your ID and password. Make yourself available on 'Ready' status. Let me know if you face any problem,' she instructed.

Soon I was geared up to receive my first call.

'Welcome to the Jungle,' Radhika smiled as I made myself available on Ready status.

'Jungle! What do you mean by Jungle?' I enquired.

'Well, time will tell you why we call this a Jungle,' she winked.

I wanted to question her further but she got busy attending her call. Soon the green light on my system blinked which was an indication of a new call.

I Immediately put on my headphone, closed my eyes and took a deep breath and recalled the names of all the gods which I'd ever came across in my entire life. Slowly I moved the cursor on the 'Accept' icon. My hands were trembling like anything.

Before the customer could speak anything, I parroted my introduction.

'Thank you for calling Finger Home. This is Scott. How may I assist you?'

But to my surprise, there was no reply from the other side.

I repeated my lines. 'Thank you…'

Still, there was no reaction. I was not sure what had gone wrong. I thought that due to noise pollution I was unable to hear so I pressed the headphone against my ears. The results remained the same. I was clueless.

'Don't worry, the call got disconnected,' Radhika said.

'Why didn't you respond?' She queried.

'I did, but I couldn't hear anything,' I shrugged.

'What! Let me check the settings,' she said and started checking the connections. She got the answer.

'You've connected the headphone in the incorrect socket. Now I've fixed it,' she informed me, twining the wire of her headphone.

'Thanks,' I replied.

That was an advantage of sitting next to an experienced player. I felt bad for the poor customer but couldn't continue for long as my phone blinked once again.

'Thank you for calling Finger Home. This is Scott. How may I assist you?'

'Hey Scott. This is Steve. How are you?' the customer introduced himself.

'I am fine. How about you?' I asked.

'Hey, I am good. Just wanted to verify whether you people have updated my new address on my account or not?' he asked.

I knew how to handle such calls as I had mugged up my training manuals. After verifying his details I provided the current address on his account. He was elated as it was his current address.

'Is there anything else I could assist you with?' I asked

'No buddy. Thanks for your help. I really appreciate it,' he said and disconnected the call.

It was a splendid call keeping in mind that it was my first direct interaction with any American. I was back on cloud nine. Mission accomplished.

'Congratulations!' Radhika said, sensing my glee.

I wanted to share my joy with Tamanna but she was preoccupied with her call. I just gave a thumbs up to show my triumph. She just beamed in reply.

'…but don't smile so much,' Radhika warned me.

I didn't like it.

'Why does she have a problem with my success?' I scowled.

Before I could say anything I got my next call. The moment I introduced myself the first thing customer probed was, 'Where are you located?'

I was not prepared for this so I requested 'Wh… what Sir?'

'Where are you located, you idiot?'

'Your call has been routed to India…' I replied.

All hell broke loose the moment I stated India.

'India…what the fuck! You guys are eating our jobs…' The customer kept on yelling abuses. I was in complete disarray. This customer was ill-treating me and my country and the best I could do was to apologize.

'I am sorry Sir…' I muttered.

'Hey, don't call me Sir. My name is Roy Sapan. Call me Roy,' he roared.

'OK…OK Sir, sorry, Mr Sapan,' I replied anxiously.

His incessant rebuking made me forget my training lessons that we needed to refer to Americans by their last name and should refrain using words like sir.

He was looking for his account balance.

'May I have your SSN?' I asked, wiping sweat off my forehead.

'Why do you need my SSN? I don't want to give my SSN to you Indians. I just want to know the balance in my account,' he yelled.

I was sure that he'd caught his wife cheating on him and to vent out his anger he called me. I couldn't go against the process flow just to please him so I dared to apprise him about the same.

'I apologize, but without the SSN I won't be able to assist you with the balance information,' I said.

All hell broke loose the moment I refused to acknowledge his demand.

'What? How dare you say no to me you fucking Indian? Just transfer to someone who can speak better English,' he screamed.

'Am I not speaking English?' I thought.

Before I could speak, he howled once again, 'Transfer the call to your manager. I will ensure this to be your last day in the company,' he threatened.

To face something like that and that too on the second call of your life was horrendous. I didn't know what to do now.

Looking at my stressed face, Radhika instantly put her call on hold and enquired, 'What happened? An irate customer?'

I nodded in response.

'Don't worry. I'll talk to him. Just hold on a sec,' she said as she released the mute button on her call.

'Thank you for being on hold. I would request you to call back as my system has hung. I apologize for the inconvenience caused,' she said and within a second she put herself on 'Away' status.

'What is he looking for?' she questioned.

'His account balance and my manager,' I stammered.

'OK. Just inform him that you are transferring the call to your manager and that's me. I know how to tackle such customers,' she winked.

'But…'

Before I could say anything she said, 'Just do what I told you.'

'OK,' I replied.

'Kindly be on hold. I am transferring the call to my manager,' I informed the customer.

'Thank you, ass!' he replied.

Immediately she seized the headphone from my hand.

'Chill. Here comes Radhika's magic,' she said as she pressed the answer button.

'Hi, This is Alias. I apologize on behalf of Scott. How may I assist you?' she introduced herself.

I was both skeptical and worried on how she would handle a 'beast' caller like him but I soon got my answer. The way she was smiling clearly indicated that she was able to transform a beast into a goat. For me it was sheer magic on call.

The way she handled the entire situation was beyond words. Though it was against the company policy to fib on calls, still she did it just to save my ass. I'm sure what she did that day only a few would dare to attempt. I would always remain thankful for her benevolence.

I needed a short break to rejuvenate myself.

I made myself on 'Not Ready' status the moment Radhika ended the call. It's strange how life changes in seconds. Just a call earlier I was on cloud nine, and the very next call brought me back to ground reality.

'Man, this job is tough,' I thought. Now I knew why Radhika called it a jungle and why she warned me not to be content with only one call. You have to be extra vigilant while tracking in the jungle as you never know when you come face to face with beasts like tigers or lions. The same goes for calling as well; this customer was like a starving lion who wanted to kill me at any cost.

I went straight to the break area to grab a cup of coffee. I needed some time off to get out of the trauma. I was disappointed at being heckled by the customer for being an Indian. I had never felt so much humiliation ever in my life. I was so shaken by the entire experience that I even forgot to thank Radhika for her selfless act.

'Can I join you?' I heard a soft voice. It was Radhika.

'You!' I said.

'Yes, me. You should have at least thanked me,' she complained in a mocking manner.

'Oh…I'm really sorry.'

'That's fine. I was just joking. Shall I join you?' she smiled.

'Sure,' I replied.

'Hope you got the answer why I said not to smile,' she said.

'Yes,' I replied sipping my coffee.

'But you know the way customer was bullying me. I just can't define it…' I could feel a lump in my throat.

'You know what? If I'd have been in your place my reply would be this,' she said and showed her middle finger and started laughing.

I was startled by her gesture as I didn't expect a female to behave like that. I'd been born and lived my entire life except for the past three months in a small town where this kind of behaviour was unthinkable.

Before I could react she provided her justification.

'First of all I would like to clear a few of your misconceptions. The customer was abusing 'Scott' and not you, so stop taking it to heart. Secondly, not all customers behave like him; only a few try to dampen your spirits. It was your bad luck that you got an irate customer so early,' she said.

'…and if by chance any customer acts rudely then we have an option to disconnect the call. But if you have to continue with the irate customer you can retort too,' she continued.

'Really?' I asked excitedly.

'Yes. The only thing you need to do is to press the mute button. That's what we all do here,' she winked.

'Oh. I got it,' I said, my excitement washed away.

'Thank you. Now I'm feeling better,' I said.

'That's what I am here for, my child,' she grinned as she patted me on my back.

'Friends?' I asked as I moved my hand towards her for a handshake.

'Sure!' she gave me a firm handshake in reply.

At that moment, I was convinced that I'd made a friend for life.

Dinner Time in the Cafe

'…the moment I said India he went berserk,' I was sharing my nightmare encounter with Tamanna and Prashant.

'You know he even asked me to transfer the call to someone who could speak better English, as if I was talking to him in some alien language,' I said in exasperation.

'What happened next?' Tamanna asked inquisitively.

'Nothing much. After battering me throughout the call he instructed me to transfer the call to my supervisor, which I did,' I replied.

'But thanks to Radhika she saved the day for me.' I apprised them how nattily she handled the situation for me.

'I have asked her to join our group. I hope it's OK with you both,' I said.

'Trust me she is really good at heart, but in case you have any problem please let me know right now,' I said.

'I'm more than happy,' Prashant smirked.

I didn't want to upset Tamanna at any cost so I ensured that the final decision was taken by her. I used an old method of emotional blackmail. Rather than informing them about my decision to include her in our circle, I tossed the ball in her court to take the final call. This would create confusion in her mind and she would give her consent in your favour.

'O…OK. Even I don't have any problem.' she murmured.

'She would be here any moment,' I said.

Within five minutes Radhika joined us at the dinner table.

'Radhika, she's Tamanna and he's Prashant,' I introduced.

It was nice to see two females shaking hands without any ego hassles. Well, it was Prashant who looked more enthusiastic in shaking hands with Radhika.

'Hi! I'm Prashant. Welcome to our group,' he introduced himself even though I had already introduced him just a moment ago.

Even though Radhika was no match with Tamanna in the looks department, but for other guys she was still a female. Maybe because I liked Tamanna, I was underestimating all other females in front of her.

'Would you like to have something?' he asked Radhika.

'No…nothing,' she replied.

'Let me get a Pepsi for the lady,' he said and walked towards the outlet in the cafeteria.

Asshole! He'd never offered me anything till then. In fact it was I who always had to pay for his extravagance in then cafe. But females have an ability to make anything possible.

The moment the two girls started discussing their nail polish brands, I was assured that things would go smoothly at least for some time if not for eternity. Even though it was rare, but I was pleased to see them together

Party Blooper

It had been over a month since the 'Go Live' day. Life had not changed much for me, in fact it had become more demanding than ever. There were only two things which comprised my daily routine, either calling, or sleeping. This calling profile had even started showing its ill effects on my day-to-day life. There were times when Rohit had to shake me awake so that I stopped reciting my introductory lines in my sleep. According to him it was creepy to sleep alongside me. Earlier I used to think that a calling job was all fun but after becoming a part of it, I had started admiring people from this industry even more.

I was still getting my daily doses of venom from some odd customers. It's just that now I had become habituated to it and it didn't trouble me any more. Every week Varun shared the last week's scores with the new associates, and as expected the gap between my and Tamanna's scores was as wide as the Pacific Ocean. Even Prashant was doing okay in terms of call scores. Among the lot of 20-odd people Tamanna was the only one who scored perfect bulls eyes twice. For me, to imagine a bulls eye score was like finding a lake in the middle of the Sahara.

'Are you upset with your scores?' Tamanna asked me on Same Time.

Same Time was an official chat service where an employee could chat with other employees for official purposes only. But 99 per cent of the time the service was being used for personal purposes only—gossip to be precise. We were not at all worried whether any other applications were down or not working but if anything happened to ST it was like experiencing a heart attack. Everybody, including the people from the management would vex IT helpdesk head till the time it got rectified. Unofficially, ST was the lifeline of the employees in We Guest.

'No, not much…' I wrote.

'One day you will definitely score better than me,' she typed, to boost my confidence.

'Ya…one day L. By the way you wanted to share some news with me,' I said.

'Oh yes. I forgot. You know what? Somebody's following me on Orkut,' she wrote.

'What?' I enquired.

'Yesterday I received a message from an anonymous person stating that he wanted to befriend me,' she wrote.

'So…?' I asked.

'So what? Just want to find him. He's from our batch only,' she wrote.

'How you can be so sure of this?' I questioned.

'He mentioned that he saw me on our induction day and even admired my beauty J' she wrote.

Her J made me green-eyed from head to toe. I felt like getting inside the chat box and giving her a tight smack. In fact, I wanted to punch this anonymous person who was trying to get close to 'My GIRL.'

'Just stay away from these roadside Romeos. They'd do anything to grab the attention of pretty girls like you. Bastards!' I wrote, venting out my resentment.

'Somebody is getting jealous J lol,' she replied.

I'd never hated J so much ever in my life. I really wanted to strangle this smiley to death. But to my bad luck, the creator of the smiley hadn't added a neck to it so there was no way anyone could strangle it.

'Who? You mean me? Come on!' I wrote.

'Well, I hardly know anybody other than you two, so you people need to help me,' she wrote.

'OK, will do that for you,' I replied.

Well, the reality was that I was keener than her to figure out this nameless person who dared to send messages to her. I was dying to meet him in person.

'Well, keep me posted when he sends a message the next time,' I mentioned.

'OK dear J' she replied.

I wished I could have forbade the usage of emoticons in the office. For the first time it looked so childish to use.

I knew whom to contact in situations like these. My man of the moment was none other than Prashant.

'Hi Prat. Are you free or on call?' I ST'd him.

'Wait, on call,' he replied.

'OK, once you're free ST me,' I wrote.

I got busy with my call.

'After finishing this call come to the meeting room. Tushar (our floor manager) wants to announce something important,' one of the supervisors whispered in my ear.

'OK,' I nodded.

'Now what happened? Will they ask me to leave the company because of my consistent low scores? No, I could see him informing the other associates as well including Tamanna,' I thought.

'Do you have any idea?' I animatedly asked Radhika.

'No, dear,' she shrugged.

There was no point talking to Prashant as I was sure even he would be clueless about the meeting. Shortly, we gathered inside Tushar's cabin for the announcement.

Tushar was one of the few good-looking guys in We Guest; that's what I had heard from my female colleagues. I had even heard that he took part in Gladrags Manhunt 2002, however, was not sure how much truth there was in it. Being a senior manager in the company is an added benefit. Every guy in the process wanted to be in his place because of his ability to make any female go weak in her knees. The only downside I could see was that he was married, if one thinks from a female's perspective. However, it was a real blessing for guys like me.

'Hello guys. Do you know why we have assembled here?' He asked, spinning the pen between his fingers. Nobody responded except looking at each other's blank faces.

'Well, nothing to worry about. It's party time, folks. Our process party has been scheduled for the coming Sunday at a pub in NOIDA. So here's your chance to have fun,' he proclaimed.

'Wow!' everybody shrieked, and our faces glowed.

I was one of the few unfortunate ones who had never been to any nightclub in his life, only knowing whatever I had seen in movies. It would be my first ever experience and unfortunately it would turn out to be the most forgettable one.

'We would definitely have a blast there!' Prashant said excitedly as we returned to our desk.

'I need to get a new dress for myself,' Radhika added.

'What for?' I asked startled.

'For the party of course,' she beamed.

'Me too,' Tamanna said.

'Wow, that's great,' I replied pursing my lips.

I have always shopped for new clothes either during the festive seasons or when there was a dire requirement. I never ever dreamt of buying clothes just to attend a single party.

'Should I get new clothes for myself as well?' I asked Prashant

'You should, idiot. After all, it's one day where we get to intermingle with other females on the floor,' he said with a lusty gleam in his eyes.

I guess he meant that here was my opportunity to get physical with female colleagues. I could see all of them daydreaming about the party.

Between all that I forgot to inform Prashant about the Orkut incident.

As only a couple of days were left, everybody on the floor got busy planning for the party. Whether it was break time or dinner time, one could hear people chatting about the party. And on top of it, there were a few mentally challenged—mostly females—who despite being on call would discuss the party animatedly.

Even I was eager for the party, but to match such serious cases was beyond my imagination.

I bought a white shirt for the party. Even though Prashant advised me to get a round party hat for myself I decided to stick with the shirt only. I didn't want anybody to gossip later that they saw a monkey with a hat in the party. We had all decided to wear something white in common.

The schedule for the party was that we all would reach office first and from there we would head towards the disc in Noida.

It was my first ever party so I wanted to look good in front of others, especially Tamanna. I put on my white shirt that cost me around 1,600 rupees without perceiving that it was the first and the last time I'd be wearing it. Had I known this I wouldn't have spent so much on this shirt.

Shortly, I reached my pick-up point to wait for the cab. I was getting desperate to reach office as I was dying to see Tamanna in her party avatar. Suddenly I felt something on the top of my head: a goddamn pigeon had crapped on my head. I never felt so deprived of not having wings in life now than ever. If I had wings at least I could make the pigeon pay for the blooper, but I couldn't do anything. I was in a desperate state and had no time to go back and change as the cab could reach any moment. It seemed my party was over even before it started.

To save my ass from further embarrassment I bought a mineral water bottle and washed the bird's droppings from my pate. My carefully designed spiky hairstyle became a casualty of this. Then speedily I dried my hair using my handkerchief as I could see the cab approaching. Before boarding the cab I tried to smell but it seemed that the cologne which I'd applied earlier was justifying its price. I acted as if nothing had happened and even though it looked weird I ensured that it appeared like I had a new hairstyle for the party. I could see a few eyebrows being raised in the cab once I took my seat at the back but nobody uttered a word. And we headed for the office.

Prashant and Radhika were already there waiting for me in the office.

At first I didn't recognize Radhika. She'd got a ponytail and for unknown reasons had applied pink blush on her cheeks, looking more like war paint. She was wearing a white off-the-shoulder top with a matching black skirt. The beaded pearlescent necklace dangling from her neck was adding to her weird appearance. Overall, for a change she was looking like a female.

On the other hand Prashant would have looked smart had he selected some shirt other than a flowery printed shirt. He looked more like a gardener than a partygoer.

'Hi br. Looking great!' Prashant sang out as he hugged me. He was behaving like a lunatic.

'You too!' I grinned.

'What about me?' Radhika enquired swaying her body.

'Just amazing. I didn't know you could look so beautiful,' I replied.

Her face lit up with the compliment. I really didn't want to spoil their mood by revealing my feeling that both of them were actually looking wonky.

'Where is Tamanna?' I asked.

'Here I am,' someone patted my shoulder.

As I looked back just one word came out of my mouth, 'WOW!' I gaped.

Tamanna was in front of me. She wore a light blue maxi dress along with floral head gear. She had applied light blue eye shadow identical to the colour of her dress. Her light pink lipstick added to her sensuality. It's well said that the lips are one of the most sensual parts of a woman's body and play a critical role in human sexual attraction. I was not sure about others, but I was sexually attracted towards her at that moment. In short she was looking stunning. As for the white colour code she was wearing a white and-black coloured triangle stretch bracelet on her left hand.

'Shut your mouth, dear,' Prashant whispered in my ear.

'Oh…' I replied trying to calm down.

'What do you think about me?' Tamanna enquired with a devious smile.

'The most beautiful woman I have ever seen in my life,' I murmured.

'Come on!' she giggled.

'No, seriously. I mean it,' I said.

She didn't answer and instead got busy talking to Radhika. Not sure whether she ignored my words intentionally or not.

'Can you come with me for a minute?' I asked Prashant.

'Where?'

'Restroom. Need to talk something important,' I replied.

We asked the girls to wait for us in the lobby as we moved towards the restroom.

'I'm thinking of proposing to her today after the party. What do you think?' I divulged my plan while stroking my hair.

'Well, I think you should wait for the right moment,' he replied, wiping his face with the tissue paper.

'If not today then when?' I questioned anxiously.

'Well…' Before he could finish his sentence my cell phone rang.

It was Tamanna, literally hollering, 'Where the hell are you people? Everyone's moving out so hurry up.'

'OK…coming,' I murmured.

'Let's go brother, otherwise the girls will kill us,' I said, completely overlooking that Prashant wanted to tell something grave about my proposal plan. I just strode out of the restroom with Prashant following me to the reception area.

Soon we all were heading to the disc. All through the journey I kept staring at Tamanna. It was not merely sexual arousal; somewhere I believed that I wouldn't be able to love any other girl more than her.

We all reached the disc around 7 p.m. We all had to wait in a queue for verification of our identity before we could enter. While waiting for our turn to get inside I saw some of my colleagues in really weird attire. Not sure whether Ashok was aware that it was a process party and not his wedding day, because it looked like he had donned his bridal *sherwani* once again. Our popular guy Manish was wearing attire resembling that of Amitabh Bachchan in the famous song '*Sara Zamana*' from the movie *Yarana*. Only the bulbs were replaced by yellow-coloured florescent spots on his dress which would give a similar effect in the dark. At least it would be easy to locate him inside the pub. Sanjay on the other hand had a mixture of both bridal and club wear. He was wearing a white *kurta* over dark blue jeans. The more you looked around the more confusing it was.

A tall beefy guy who must be around seven feet in height with biceps measuring more than the size of my thigh was verifying our details. Prashant later informed me that these king-size bulldozers in the shape of humans work as bouncers in nightclubs and if anybody misbehaves, they know how to handle them. I wonder who would even dare to think of misbehaving in front of these monsters. This guy could easily pick me up with one of his hands and throw me like a dart. Just standing in front of these guys could bring a drunken person's senses back to normal. I was sure that the major portion of their salaries was spent on their diet only.

Soon my turn arrived.

'Your name and Employee ID?' he asked.

'Shiv and 108,' I replied. He searched for my name and marked a tick against it.

'Show me your hand,' he said.

'For what?' I asked as I pushed my hand towards him.

I got my answer as put a stamp on my wrist as an authorization that I could enter the disc without any further hindrance. When I looked at it closely it had the logo of the disc on it.

Apart from a few coloured neon lights it was almost dark inside the disc. It took a few minutes for my eyes to adapt to the dim light. In a little while I checked out the settings. The dance area was located in the middle of the floor. On its right side there was a raised platform known as the DJ cube where a bald DJ was playing some music which was totally alien to me. Later I was informed that it was trance music. The only thing I could relate myself with the bald DJ was the headphone he had around his neck. I wonder whether he too needed to make calls while playing music. The seating arrangements were on the left hand side of the floor where a few comfortable couches were placed. I could see that a few of my colleagues had already booked the corner seats. The bar was located on the extreme left of the room. It was the most lit up area in the entire floor. The shelves on the rear had many expensive liquor bottles laid out. However, I later came to know that those expensive brands were showpieces only and we wouldn't be getting an opportunity to get a taste of them. Our 'Unlimited booze' was restricted to some low-priced brands only.

We seized the couch near the dance floor. All together it was a different world. I had never been to heaven, but it was like the scenes I had seen in mythological movies where beautiful *apsaras* were dancing and men were enjoying their drinks all the time without any specific reason.

I didn't know that these process parties could bring so much transformation exclusively among females; even after working for more than a month in the process it was a herculean task to identify even a single female of my process.

'Man! Just look at Deepika. She is looking so…hot. Just look at those thighs,' Prashant mumbled, ensuring that the girls with us didn't hear it. He was quite aware of the fact that praising a hot girl like Deepika would have an adverse effect. As a consequence we might end up dancing all alone on the floor like a gay couple.

'What happened? Why you are grinning so much?' Tamanna queried.

'No…nothing. It's just guy talk,' I replied.

'I know you people, especially Prashant. I saw you checking Deepika out with those lusty eyes,' Radhika squealed, pointing to Prashant.

Thank God she hadn't taken my name as I didn't want my image of mama's boy or the boy next door to take a beating. One should've seen Prashant's face; it looked as if his father had caught him watching porn and wanted an explanation. It seemed he'd start howling any moment. Only God could tell how she got to know what we were chatting.

'I…I didn't…' Prashant stammered.

'It's OK. I don't need an explanation!' Radhika replied with a straight face.

'Hey, lets have something,' I tried to change the topic.

'Good idea. It's better to get the drinks before it gets jam-packed there,' Tamanna pointed to the bar.

'The boys will do the honours for us,' Radhika beamed.

'Sure. We'll get the drinks,' I replied.

In the meantime Prashant kept mum, not sure whether he'd be able to get over the shock of being labeled a filthy person.

'So what would you like to have?' I questioned.

'Beer for me,' Radhika chuckled.

'And for you?' I looked at Tamanna.

'I want to have vodka with orange juice,' she smiled.

Being raised in a conservative family, I didn't expect the girls to be so bold about having alcohol. But maybe it was time for me to get acclimatized with the changes. If they could work along with us and earn, they had an equal right to drink too, I thought.

We both got up from our seats and walked towards the bar.

'Cheer up, buddy. The world has not ended. It happens,' I said, trying to raise Prashant's spirits.

'Even though she heard it, she should have kept it to herself,' he grumbled.

'I know, but let bygones be bygones,' I said as I swung my right arm around his shoulders.

'But you know Deepika is really looking *Hot*.'. I sighed.

'You bastard!' he cursed and burst out in laughter.

As we moved towards the bar somebody embraced me from behind. I knew that 'someone' was a female for obvious reasons. Men don't have boobs.

It was Puja who was holding me; I got to know the moment I turned towards her.

What the fuck was she wearing? Everybody in the company knew that she liked to show her curvaceous 'S backwards' figure (according to her), but actually it was a bloated 'S backwards' figure. But I guess that day she had crossed all limits. Her boobs were easily visible through the transparent white top she was wearing. Not sure whether she purposely missed out wearing her bra.

'Hello guys!' she greeted us with an impish smile.

'Hi Puja. Good to see you,' I replied, trying my best not to look at her chest.

I don't know what happened; I still remember that we hardly talked to each other on the floor apart from greeting each other during log-in hours, but she hugged me and planted a kiss on my cheek.

I shoved her a bit as I was upset by her act. I could smell that she was already in high spirits.

'She's already drunk,' Prashant whispered.

'I can smell that,' I replied with irritation.

Even though it was a kiss from a female, I didn't expect it, at least from Puja. I would have liked my first kiss to be a memorable one but it turned out to be most forgettable. She should have been aware of my reputation as a one-woman man.

I immediately pulled out my hanky and rubbed off the lipstick marks on my cheek. I didn't want any traces of lipstick so scoured it for a good five minutes.

Now it was Prashant's turn to snigger. He couldn't stop laughing at my misery.

'For God's sake don't speak a word about this in front of Tamanna. Otherwise my dream of becoming her boyfriend will remain a dream forever,' I muttered.

He just nodded in reply as he kept sniggering.

Puja vanished in no time, the same way she'd appeared a few moments back. I was feeling pity for her next target.

It had been only five minutes since the bar had started serving liquor but it already looked like a beehive. Not sure how Puja got her drink. Maybe a lecher like Sanjay had helped her.

Somehow we managed to reach the bar by squeezing through the mob. At that moment my colleagues' behaviour could easily be that of an unruly mob. The only difference was that here the mob was trying to get hold of glasses of their favoured alcohol, and that too for free.

'I need vodka with orange juice and another one with whisky and coke,' I almost screamed.

It was really tough to hold my place there as everyone wanted to be served first. Not sure how many kicks I had to endure there. Even though it was my first trip to a night club, I noticed that a nightclub has different parameters of serving liquor to its patrons especially when it's an 'unlimited booze and food' party. The bartender very cleverly (may be instructed to do so) served only that much liquor which was good enough to get a feel of liquor and not more than that. It seemed as if the bartender had to pay from his pocket.

Soon we grasped our drinks and returned to the couch. It was more challenging to hold on to the drink than to walk over a rope tied between the two buildings on our way back.

'Here's your vodka,' I passed over the glass to Tamanna.

Prashant passed over the beer to Radhika who was writhing listening to the loud music. The weird thing was that she was doing this while sitting on the couch.

'Long live our friendship!' we all screamed and clinked the glasses.

'For my love (in silence),' I thought.

I was flabbergasted to see Tamanna downing her entire glass of vodka in one go. It showed that she was a veteran drinker. It was hard to digest her new avatar, especially due to the way she carried herself in the office.

I too got carried away and swigged my glass in one breath. May be my so-called male ego couldn't digest the fact that if a female could do this then why couldn't I.

'That's like my Tiger!' Prashant applauded while sipping his beer.

But I instantly realized it was not a good idea to lock horns with a veteran. At times it's better to overlook your male ego. It was my first mistake of the day. Drinking an entire glass of whisky in one go and that too on an empty stomach was too much for an inexperienced player like me.

I guess the bartender had forgotten to apply the 'feel of alcohol' policy to my drink.

It felt like an asteroid had hit me hard. My head started to spin.

'Are you all right?' Radhika quizzed looking at my grimace.

'Ya…yes, I'm all right,' I stammered.

I could see Prashant sniggering at my plight. He sensed my first mistake of the day. Suddenly I could hear the trance track being changed to a more familiar Hindi track suggesting it was time to jig.

Everybody started bustling towards the dance floor. Prashant was the first to join them. Soon Radhika joined him.

'Are you coming?' Tamanna quizzed.

'You go. I'll join you in five minutes.' I replied.

'Are you sure?' She looked concerned.

'Ya…you go. I'm just feeling a bit tipsy so just need a couple of minutes,' I grinned.

I cursed myself for competing with a seasoned drinker like Tamanna but the damage had been done and I could only wait for get the effect to diminish.

I was envious of Prashant who was dancing then with two attractive girls including Tamanna. I didn't know from where I gathered all my strength and dragged myself towards the dance floor. Maybe the very thought of Tamanna dancing with other males who almost turn into perverts during parties made me feel insecure.

But my bad luck was in full play. I could see Tushar approaching us with a glass of whiskey. He too joined the group. Though he was just enjoying, but when your manager starts shaking a leg with you, you need to be vigilant. Your girl might join him and trust me that would be a dreadful sight.

I managed to stand—in the state I was in the only thing I could do was to stand—in-between 'My girl' and 'My manager', but suddenly my manager offered me his drink. It was my first job and in no case would I have liked to offend my manager, so despite being tipsy I accepted his offer. I gulped the whole glass. It was the second blunder of the day. Within minutes Tushar disappeared from the scene. Soon the whisky showed its true colours. I felt nauseated and to save myself from further embarrassment I decided to retire to the couch again. It was too much for me to even stand there for a minute so I slouched to the couch leaving Tamanna all alone on the dance floor. I almost tripped while returning but somehow managed to control myself.

Though I was inebriated, my eyes roved around.

Ashok the nose digger instead of dancing was actually trampling the dance floor. He even tried his best to get close to the female crowd but disappointment followed him everywhere. It was hilarious to see girls disappearing the moment they saw him approaching. Sanjay, being dizzy at the moment started to swing his *kurta* around in the air, but not for long. As soon as one of the bouncers walked towards him, he put his *kurta* back on, wisely, I think. I didn't see him on the dance floor after that.

Deepika was looking extremely sexy in her short black dress but it seemed that she was only interested in grabbing Tushar the manager's attention. Even though there were other lunatics who'd do anything for her, at least today, she only followed Tushar. Once Tamanna told me that she liked Tushar for his looks, but I think it was more due to his position as the manager.

'Have it: it'll make you feel better,' Somebody muttered in my ear.

Tamanna and Prashant were standing in front of me with a slice of lemon.

How much she cares for me, and here I acted like a corny guy, I thought.

She returned to the dance floor. It was a startling experience to watch her dancing. I could see her hair fluttering in the air and it was a true delight to see that.

Because everybody was busy dancing, I was in charge of taking care of their belongings, bags and cell phones. I really wanted to check her messages but somehow felt reluctant to do that.

'What if she gets to know of it? She'd really get upset and then she might even stop talking to me. But here was a golden chance to know whether she had a boy friend or not.' I pondered on the options available.

They say nobody can find what's going inside a woman's mind, but I'm sure a female's mobile could easily divulge some if not all truths, but the real challenge was to get hold of it. You'd hardly find a female and her mobile apart. They always keep their mobiles close to their chests the way kangaroos do with their children.

Here I was holding her mobile and I really didn't want to miss my one–in-a-million chance. But I wanted to ensure that nobody was around. I could see Tamanna busy dancing with Radhika and Prashant. I had given strict instructions to Prashant that being his sister-in-law—Prashant being my friend first, Tamanna being my girl, logically would be his sister-in-law—he should safeguard her on the floor.

Before I could do anything, Tamanna's mobile blinked. With much reluctance I looked at the screen. Some Amit's name was flashing.

'Who could be this Amit, a boyfriend? Brother?' I thought.

'Maybe her brother is calling in to enquire about her—but she only has a sister, then who is this Amit?' I thought.

'Should I call her or answer myself?' As I was thinking about my next step the call ended. Now I really wanted to know about this Amit who'd called her so late. Without wasting any time I quickly clicked her message inbox but to my bad luck it was password protected.

'Shit!' That's what I could utter.

Once again a man's attempt to know what's inside a female's mind failed wretchedly.

Between all that I forgot to keep an eye on Tamanna. As I lifted my head I could see Tamanna scowling at me with hands on her hips. Now I was dead. She'd caught me red-handed.

'I…I'm sorry,' I stammered. I could see her face sweating as if she'd just returned from a walk in 45º C temperature.

'Were you trying to peep into my messages?' she demanded. I could feel a lump in my throat.

'No…never, why should I?' I mumbled.

'Don't lie, I saw you fiddling with my mobile,' she yelled, pointing to me.

Even though she was frowning, she was still looking like a million bucks.

'I was not searching your messages, in fact I was about to call you. There was a missed call but as you were busy dancing I thought I'd attend it. If you don't trust me you can see for yourself,' I retorted in a firm tone as I handed over the cell phone to her.

She saw the missed call from Amit. One should see or test how quickly a girl's expression could change. Realizing it was a missed call, her facial expression turned from 'How dare you' to 'I am so sorry'.

'I am really sorry, Shiv,' she blubbered and hugged me.

It was a blessing in disguise. I never thought I'd get a hug from her, and that too for peeping into her mobile. I too hugged her. Trust me it was all heaven.

'Thats fine. It happens,' I replied as I kept hugging her.

Maybe because she was drunk and feeling guilty at the same time stimulated her to hug me. But I was not complaining at all. She soon became aware of the real world around us as she backed off. I wished it could have continued forever. She composed herself and returned to the couch next to me.

Instantly she changed the topic. 'Prashant is a terrific dancer,' she said, looking at him.

'Ya…he dances well,' I echoed. I didn't want to further discomfit her so I too joined the conversation though I ensured I kept looking at her expression through the corner of my eyes.

Once again her cell phone blinked. I couldn't see the caller's name but her face lit up like a 100-watt bulb.

'Really! I'm coming out!' she almost yelled.

'Hey, what happened?' I asked.

'If anyone asks for me, say I wasn't feeling well so I went home,' she replied gathering her stuff.

'Why…what happened? You're quite fine,' I said in a strained voice.

'Try to understand, I have to go,' she winked.

'What do you mean?' I knew something was terribly wrong.

'Is it something to do with Amit? What about my proposal?' I thought.

'I'm leaving dear. See you in office on Monday,' she said and strolled towards the exit.

'Wait,' I bellowed but it seemed she didn't hear and walked out.

I started to panic. She got a call from someone and that someone was waiting outside. It must be Amit. I had to check it. I sprang up from my seat and stomped off towards the exit. I didn't want to disturb Prashant so I walked alone towards the parking while making sure that she didn't notice me. I forgot that moments ago, I was feeling tipsy, but now anxiety overpowered my dizziness.

My heart was beating faster than the engine of a *Rajdhani* express. The very thought of seeing her with someone else was making my heart sink.

She should have told me earlier if she had a boyfriend. She had no right to play with my innocent heart. But on the other hand I overlooked the fact that she never made an impression ever that she was single. She was secretive like other females, but she always treated me like a friend.

Moments later my world came crashing down. I felt as if Tamanna had trampled my innocent heart under a road roller. Tears rolled down my cheeks. I was supposed to propose to her that day, and there she was embracing someone else. I was sure it was Amit cuddling 'My Girl'. My heart couldn't tolerate more so I turned back and slogged towards the disc. Tears kept on rolling down my cheeks.

The peppy song playing in the background started sounding like one of the heart-breaking songs sung by Muhammad Rafi in the Sixties. I was trembling as if somebody had betrayed me for no fault of mine. The most beautiful gift suddenly turned into the most dreadful one.

'How could she do this to me?' I thought.

'Hey, where have you been, where is Tamanna?' Prashant quizzed, a whisky in his hand.

I didn't utter a word.

'Have you done something?' I could see a mischievous smile on his face.

I felt like hitting him hard. His words felt like he was rubbing salt on my fresh wounds.

Without replying, I grabbed the whisky in his hand and finished it in one go once again.

'I want more,' I howled.

'Easy Shiv, I guess it's enough for now,' Prashant said, trying to hold me. He looked worried.

'I want more,' I repeated.

'Why? What happened, and for God's sake where's Tamanna?' he asked.

Once again I didn't answer him and slogged towards the bar after releasing myself from his grasp.

'One large whisky. Don't you dare mix anything,' I ordered pointing a finger at him.

The bartender was habitual to see gums like me so he didn't respond and just handed over the glass.

Before Prashant could stop me, I gulped the entire glass in one go and this turned out to be my final mistake for the day. It was the last nail which I myself fixed on my own coffin. My mind went blank and I didn't know what happened afterwards. I still felt sorry for all those especially Prashant who had to bear the brunt of my preposterousness. Maybe I was under the impression that the more I drank the more easily I could make myself forget Tamanna. Later on I realized it was one of the most absurd things to do in life.

The last thing I remember was that I threw up after having my final drink and the rest as they say was history. The next 24 hours were completely expunged from my memory.

The Day after the Nightmare (the Party)

'Oh God! Please help!' I woke up with excruciating pain in my head.

'I shouldn't have drunk so much,' I repented.

Suddenly I became conscious of the events which had happened the day before.

'Where the hell am I?' I thought as I roved around. The surroundings looked familiar. It was my room and I was on my bed.

'Who brought me here? What happened yesterday after I went blank?' All sorts of questions came to my mind. As I looked at the wall clock it showed 9 p.m. It meant I'd slept for almost 24 hours. Without delay I sprang out of bed and rushed towards my cell phone. I even forgot my headache.

'Fuck, 58 missed calls, 18 unread messages. Have I done something?' I was fidgeting.

The only thing I remembered was the time when I puked and had no idea what happened afterwards. As I was busy in my thoughts, Rohit entered.

'So my prince has finally woken up,' he smiled.

'Do you know what happened last night?' I asked clutching his shoulder.

'Who brought me home?' I continued before he could answer my first question.

'Your friend Prashant and other cab mates. You were not in your senses; your shirt was torn from behind. It was hard to believe at first, that it was you,' he grumbled.

I was dejected at losing my hard-earned 1,600 rupees in just one night. I had to work for almost two nights to earn this much and I lost it within three hours.

'You couldn't stand on your own. I had to get you here. The only thing I remember you kept on repeating you shouldn't have done this,' he said.

'Is everything alright?' he enquired.

'It all happened because of that bitch Tamanna. She betrayed my trust,' I said, trembling.

The breeze of love had changed direction: 'My Girl' had turned into a 'Bitch' now.

'OK, now I get it. Relax, brother. It's a BPO world and not your typical Bollywood movie where a heroine loves only one hero. Here the hero and heroine change periodically. You need to get used to it,' he lectured.

'I know.' I still couldn't get rid of the scene when she hugged that asshole. Once again tears were rolling down my cheeks.

'Come on, grow up. Don't behave like a teenager,' he said wiping tears off my cheeks.

'Anyways, do call Prashant. He needs to talk something urgent to you and meanwhile I'll get a cup of tea for you,' he said, moving towards the kitchen.

I was feeling fretful but with no options left I dialed his number as I wanted to know what I did the other night.

Before I could utter a word he screamed 'You bastard, why were you not picking up my call? Do you have any idea what happened yesterday?'

'That's why I called you,' I mumbled.

'Tushar wants to talk to you on Monday,' he said.

'I got this job after so much pain and now I am about to lose it. Fuck,' I thought.

'Man, you showed your true colours last night. Everyone was surprised to see you in that avatar,' he laughed.

'Just tell me what I did!' I shouted.

'Do you remember when I asked you about Tamanna's whereabouts?' he asked.

'Yes I do,' I answered.

'You just went berserk after that. After you puked the first time you rushed towards the dance floor even though I tried to stop you. Instead of dancing you puked on the floor which scared off the others present there. You even tried to grab Tushar's drink but he refused, seeing your condition. You then kept nagging him big time. And to top it all you even broke a few glasses there. Man, it was a total fiasco. Nobody knew what happened to you,' he said.

'Even the bouncers had a hard time controlling you. They even carried you out so that fresh air could relax you but you kept on hitting them all through. Man, you have some guts.'

'What happened then'? I asked.

'You just plopped on the staircase and dozed off. But that's not the end of the story. As you were feeling thirsty I went inside to get water, and you just vanished from the scene. I sprinted towards the main gate. There, one of the cab drivers told me that he saw someone lying in the pit adjacent to the main road. It was a big respite to locate you there. Later on the same cab driver helped me pick you up from the pit and put you inside the cab. Trust me it was a humiliating experience.'

I didn't know what to say after hearing all that. I couldn't believe I'd stooped so low in life, but I guess it was because I plunged into the trap called love. On the other hand I was thankful to Prashant for all that he did for me. He even spoiled his evening just to make sure I was safe.

'Thank you.' That's all I could utter. I was blubbering.

'Nope. Anything for you, bro,' he replied.

'What about Radhika? Did she say anything? Not sure how I'll make eye contact with her on Monday.' I heaved a sigh.

'Well, it's not only Radhika: you have to face the entire floor on Monday,' he said.

'Shit! I didn't take that into account,' I grumbled. It would be a dreadful situation to face everyone on Monday.

I was surprised he didn't raise a query when I didn't enquire about Tamanna 'the Bitch' but soon I got the answer.

'I did talk to Tamanna afterwards, and I knew what provoked you to do all this,' he murmured.

'Good that you got to know. I was about to tell you,' I said in a firm voice.

'I want to say something,' he said timidly.

'Sure; after all, you saved my life, bro,' I said.

'I knew about Tamanna's boyfriend Amit,' he exploded a bomb.

'What?' I was flabbergasted.

'You knew about that asshole and still kept it secret. Why didn't you tell me?' I ranted forgetting that he'd saved me.

'After considering what happened yesterday, I should have,' he admitted.

'I'm not sure whether Tamanna ever spoke about someone stalking her on Orkut,' he asked.

'Y...yes. She *did* talk about that but somehow I forgot to tell you,' I replied.

'It was I who did all that,' he revealed.

'But why?' I shouted. 'Now don't tell me that you too were after her.'

'Fuck you, you ass. I did it for you so that I could find the truth. I was sure if she had a boyfriend I'd get to know through Orkut only,' he said.

'I tried to disclose the bitter truth in the restroom but you didn't listen and just walked out the moment Tamanna called you,' he said.

I recalled the scene where he wanted to tell me something about my plan for proposing but I'd just walked out.

'You should have stopped me. At least that would have been better than lying lifelessly in the pit,' I said remorsefully.

'Anyway, no point crying over spilt milk. Let's wait for Monday and see what Tushar has decided about my future,' I shuddered.

'Tamanna wants to talk to you...' he murmured.

'Do you have anything else to talk?' My obstinate tone was enough to hint that Tamanna 'The Bitch' was now a closed chapter of my life.

Now I was really plagued thinking about Tushar's decision whether he'd keep me or kick me out of the company. I was praying that I hadn't transgressed too much last evening and he'd take into account that this was my first behavioral issue of any kind in the company.

Tricked by Radhika

It had been three months since we had that nightmarish process party but it still haunted me in my dreams. The day after the party was the most excruciating day of my life when I had to face umpteen uncomfortable questions from cab drivers, guards on duty, dept line HR and finally my manager Tushar. I could never forget the time when Tushar called me to enquire and wanted to know exactly what happened to me that other night. Due to embarrassment I just stood with my head hanging in front of him just like when as kids we used to stand in front of our principal when we had done something wrong. In such situations you wished you'd never been born in the first place and if by chance you were born you wished to be deaf and dumb.

The only thing which I considered positive was that my hiring manager Rahul Sati had joined another organization in Pune as a senior manager so I did not have to face him. I'd never have returned had I known he was still in the company. Till this day guys from the other processes taunt about my lunatic behaviour in the party. At times I felt like breaking their jaws but had to control my emotions. Another warning letter meant I was out of the company. I'd been given a lifeline only because Tushar argued with HR on my behalf otherwise HR was adamant at terminating me. But one thing was obvious: I'd become quite popular in the entire We Guest premises. Earlier only a few people like Radhika, Prashant, Tamanna 'The Bitch' and Varun (for my constant low scores) knew me.

Life had changed a lot during those three months. HR had issued me a warning letter for my conduct and it clearly stated that management would observe my conduct for the next six months and if I committed something insane again, I'd be kicked out of the company. I'd stopped talking to Tamanna 'The Bitch' even though she tried her best to explain about her lover Amit but I didn't care to listen. All the bashings post the party added fuel to my resentment against her. When you're hurt, especially in love, you start doing silly things like what we used to do in Class 5. I had issued an ultimatum to Radhika and Prashant to choose between Tamanna and me. At first I was skeptical whether they'd choose me or not, but when I blackmailed them emotionally, they decided to stick with me. At least in my presence they avoided talking to Tamanna.

'That fucking party really sent my reputation for a toss,' I said, entwining my fingers in the wires of my headphone.

'I know, but now you should stop worrying about it. It's a closed chapter, my friend. Just forget it,' Radhika said emphatically.

'I want to forget it but these bastards keep on reminding me,' I said angrily.

'I know, but the best you can do is to avoid it: simple,' Radhika said.

'Ya…you're right,' I said, pursing my lips.

'One thing…Tamanna wants to talk to you once,' she said hesitantly.

'Why? About her fucking boyfriend!' I almost screamed.

The way her eyeballs almost popped out clearly showed that she didn't like what I said.

'Sorry,'. I murmured. I shouldn't have used the word 'fucking' so vociferously.

'That's better,' she returned to normal by shrinking her eyeballs.

'Come on. It's been three months. Just talk to her once,' she said, holding my hand.

'I told you not to talk about it…' I said.

'She has resigned.' She dropped the bomb before I could add anything else.

'What! When? Why?' I bawled.

'Because of your attitude, asshole,' Radhika retorted.

'My attitude!' I shrugged.

'I think you're forgetting that she didn't disclose about her 'would be' Amit, and it's because of her only I was handed a warning letter,' I frowned.

'Not againnnnnnnnnn!' She raised her left eyebrow.

'OK, Shiv just answer me. Did she ever suggest that she had feelings for you?' she questioned.

'No, but she…' I mumbled after a minute's pause.

'But what, you asshole?' she glared. I didn't know why she kept calling me an asshole.

'But she never even shared that she was going around with someone,' I retorted.

'OK. Have you ever told her that you love her?' she quizzed as if she was a criminal lawyer in her last birth and was still carrying some of the characteristics in this life.

'I was about to…in the party,' I said, trying to justify my stand.

'Wow, that's great. You didn't reveal your feelings and expected being a girl she would share her status with the world. That's worth applauding.' She gestured as if she was clapping.

I really hated her for perplexing me.

'OK. Let's not beat around the bush. Just answer me this, whether you want Tamanna to stay here or leave?' she asked me straightforwardly.

I was not sure whether she did it because she was irritated with my replies, or just wanted to make me feel guilty.

Even though I hated Tamanna because of her 'would be' but somewhere I didn't want her to go away from my sight: after all she was my first love. Here, I must confess that at times I still stared at her clandestinely. And I didn't want to spend the rest of my life with the blame that she had to leave the company because of me. I didn't know it then, but Tamanna was the only girl whom I loved and hated the most ever in life.

'No. I don't want her to leave,' I mumbled with my head down.

'That's fine. Now I'm calling her.' She grinned.

Before I could do anything she STed her.

'Hey, there's good news for you, baby. Shiv is ready to talk to you,' she wrote.

'Meet him in 15 minutes in the cafe,' she wrote further.

'Thanks sweetie J' Tamanna replied.

'Don't you think it's too fast for a patch up?' I raised a doubt.

'No. It's not,' she replied.

There's no point arguing with the opposite sex, so I surrendered.

I really wanted the next 15 minutes to be equivalent to 15 minutes time spent on Jupiter, but because I was an inhabitant of Earth, the 15 minutes passed by as per Earth time.

I didn't want to show any resentment towards her or her 'would be' Amit. Also, I needed to be careful of my conduct otherwise another warning letter within six months meant the company's doors would be shut forever. I was not in a position to lose my job and spend another two-three months in search of another one.

I took a deep breath and walked towards the cafeteria after placing my Avaya on 'Dinner break' status.

Tamanna was standing at the entrance and greeted me the moment I made an entry. 'Hi Shiv.'

Even though she'd broken my heart in a million pieces, she was still looking lovely as usual. Once again I was awestruck to see her so close. Leaving aside Amit's incident, I still loved her, but it needed a superhuman effort to ignore that part.

'Hello,' I muttered imperturbably.

We both grabbed a corner table and sat there in complete silence. I could see her entwining her *dupatta* around her finger. Not sure what she would achieve by doing that. I also remained silent as I wanted her to start the conversation.

Through the corner of my eyes I could see her pink lipstick glistening and her earrings dangling from her ears touching her soft cheeks every time she made a movement.

We sat there for almost five minutes without uttering a single word when she finally broke the ice.

'Are you still upset?' she questioned in her usual mellow tone.

'No. Why should I? You should get 'The Miss Heartbreaker' award for breaking my innocent heart,' I thought.

I didn't reply. I was evading eye contact with her. It always made me go weak. Though I wanted to say yes, I had no courage to say so in front of her. Man, I still loved her a lot.

'Are you still upset?' she repeated.

'No,' I murmured.

'But you should have told me about your boyfriend,' I grumbled.

'I am really sorry. I wanted to, but it all got messed up. I wanted to introduce him but he insisted on catching up with all of you at some other time. Later on through Prashant I came to know what you did in the party after I left,' she answered.

'But didn't you know that I had feelings for you?' I questioned.

'I had some idea, but didn't want to lose a friend like you so I ignored it. I thought when the time would be right I would let you know,' she said.

'Just a bloody *friend*!' I exclaimed.

'What the fuck is this? Why do things like "I consider you as my friend or brother only" happen to guys like me,' I thought.

'OK, leave all this. What do you want from me?' I heaved a sigh.

'I want you to remain my friend,' she said, holding my hand. It felt like heaven once again. My heart wanted to keep on holding her hand, but my mind was dead against it. I decided to follow my mind so I pulled back.

'To be honest I don't know whether I can continue the way I was three months back, but I can try,' I replied, controlling my emotions. Her face lit up.

'But I have two conditions. First, you will never force me to meet your 'would be' Amit, and secondly, the more important one, even though you consider me as your friend, I will always love you,' I announced. She blushed but didn't say anything.

It was the first time ever that I had expressed my love to someone. Though I always wished that the women would respond in a similar manner but it didn't happen. Here, I was just a bloody *friend*. The uncanny part was that I'd expressed my love to someone who was already in love with somebody else.

'OK. Done!' she said, flashing her million-dollar smile.

'I hope now you'll take back your resignation,' I said.

'Resignation? Who? Me?' She was startled.

'Yes, of course, you. Radhika told me that you resigned because I was not talking to you,' I said.

'Nothing like that. I was upset and was missing my friend, but nothing like resigning,' she cleared.

There she goes again: *friend*. Now I had to live all my life being her friend.

'I think she tricked you so that we start talking to each other,' she said.

'I'll kill her,' I hollered.

Tamanna smiled and after a pause of a few seconds I too joined her.

Once again we all had become friends. The only difference was that this time it was crystal clear that even though I was a boy but not her 'Boyfriend': I was only a *bloody friend*. Earlier, I used to look for excuses to be in her company, but later I looked for excuses to maintain distance from her.

Prashant through his sources told me that Amit and Tamanna were a couple since their graduation days. Her boyfriend belonged to an influential business family and no prizes for guessing he would soon be joining the family business. Lucky bastard. But life is just not about a pleasant ride on a smooth road; it's full of twists and turns and the best or worst thing is that you never know when you have to face it.

Dinner with Hooligans

'Let's go for dinner,' Tamanna wrote on ST.

I was trying my best to keep a distance but destiny kept on crossing our paths. I had opted for a different shift but one of my teammates had to go on emergency leave and I was asked to fill in. Coincidently, Tamanna was doing the same shift. Prashant and Radhika were in the morning shift so it was only I who could go with her at the moment.

'I feel like eating Chinese,' she said.

'OK,' I nodded. It hardly mattered whether she wanted to eat Chinese or Indian. I just wanted to finish as soon as possible and rush back to my workstation.

Soon we two went out to grab Chinese from the roadside *dhaba*s outside. We had recently switched to eating outside at the *dhabas*. The number of *dhabas* was indirectly proportional to the taste of the food served in the cafe which was getting pathetic by the day. Sometimes I suspected that the office vendor used the same gravy for the entire week, just adding different stuff and give mouthwatering names *likes paneer do pyaza, matar paneer*, etc. But all of them tasted the same while the food prepared in the *dhabas* tasted as if it had been prepared by top chefs. Maybe we had developed a liking for food prepared in the most unhygienic conditions one could imagine. I had heard, of course through Prashant (who else?) that this Chinese van which claimed to be a specialist in Chinese food as per the hoarding sagging from its rooftop used water from the same water tank to cook food and for the toilet. Despite that one had to wait for at least 10–15 minutes to get one's order. Ironically, we still loved the food prepared by them.

It was December and winter was at its peak so not many people were eating outside. There were only a few handful of employees like us apart from *dhabawala*s and a few cab drivers snoring heavily in their cabs who could be seen outside the campus. There was one exception, a QRT (Quick Response Team) van parked a few yards away from the campus irrespective of whether the temperature was 50° or zero degrees Celsius. Their job was to provide a quick response in case of some tragedy. Fortunately, we never had an opportunity to actually experience their service till then. After looking at the frail bodies of the guards in the van it was hard to believe that they were hired to protect us. The agonizing look on their faces made you feel as if they were carrying sacks filled with sand instead of guns.

'*Bhaiyya*, two half plates of chicken chow mein and one half plate boneless chicken chilli,' Tamanna ordered.

I don't know why girls—especially pretty girls—insist on calling everyone *bhaiyya* so much. You'd find them calling everyone from guards, cab drivers or even rickshaw-pullers *bhaiyya* all the time.

'Thank God at least I was not her *bhaiyya* but a ' *friend*,' I thought.

'Do you want anything else?' she asked.

'Ask them to add a Coke.'

I didn't notice that at the table adjacent to our's there were four guys gorging *parathas*. At first I ignored them thinking that they must be from some different process but soon realized that one of them was in his boxers. Even though there wasn't any stringent rule regarding wearing formals in the office but to come to office in boxers was unacceptable. I soon got to know that they were outsiders and had no real business there. They'd turn up almost every day and stare at every female employee with lusty eyes. Being a public place the guards couldn't forbid them from eating there.

I noticed they were having alcohol as well.

'Let's get the food packed: we'll eat it inside,' I proposed.

'No, I want to eat here. Its chilling here, lets enjoy the weather,' she insisted.

'But…' I didn't know what bugged me.

Maybe I was thinking too much. There were four *dhabas*, each had at least three or four guys and on top of it we had our QRT to guard us. So I stopped worrying about them.

'I want to share something,' Tamanna said timidly.

'What?'

'Actually…things are not going well between me and Amit,' she murmured.

Though I was least interested in what was going on in her and Amit's love life, but the moment I heard the word 'not going right', I craned my neck towards her. Those three words sounded like melody to my ears.

'What happened?' I said sounding sympathetic. But in reality my heart was elated. I felt like doing a full Monty in the middle of the road.

'I don't know, but it seems it's not like what it was in the beginning,' she said, dejected.

I'd never been in a relationship and the only attempt I made was turned to 'friends only' so I couldn't comment.

I kept mum.

'Earlier he used to call me every five minutes, but I don't know why for the past few months whenever we meet it seems more like a formality than love,' she said dispiritedly.

My spirits were getting higher with each passing sentence, but I had to act as if I was really concerned about all this.

'Just leave him and come to me, my cutie!' I thought.

'This was the main reason why I didn't disclose to anyone that I had a boyfriend. I'm not sure whether he's bored with me,' she blubbered.

'Come on Tamanna. How on Earth can anyone think of getting bored of you? It's ridiculous,' I said emphatically.

'Fucking loser,' I thought of Amit.

Before we could continue with our chat someone yelled.

'What's your plan, sweetie? Come with us, we'l take you for a ride!' We craned our heads towards the sound. It was one of the four guys who'd passed the lewd comment. We could see them sniggering.

'Hey, keep your mouth shut!' Tamanna roared.

'Let's move inside the campus,' I said.

'Come on, join us here,' another other moron shouted.

Before she could retort I said, 'There's no point talking to these bastards. Let's move inside.'

'But…' she said exasperatedly.

'*Bhaiyya*, kindly do us a favor and send the food inside. We'll pay you there,' I said and started walking along with Tamanna towards the company's gate.

As we moved towards the company's entrance gate one of the pesky assholes who was gorging *parathas* suddenly charged in and blocked our way.

'I asked you something and you didn't answer!' he blurted, showing his tobacco stained teeth.

'Excuse me, don't you have manners?' Tamanna hollered, pointing at him, trembling with anger.

'Sir, I request you to let us go.' I requested.

I didn't want to retort even though I felt like smacking him but at that point I just wanted to get inside the entrance gate along with Tamanna as soon as possible.

'If I don't allow, then…' he guffawed.

One Tight Slap!

Before I could react Tamanna did the inevitable. She dazed the entire public standing there including me by evincing her true guts. One should have seen the hooligan's face, his face turned red in no time and any moment I could envisage him wailing like a toddler. I wish I had a camera handy so that I could capture the moment and show the entire world that if you misbehave with any female this would be the result. This was my Kodak moment of the night.

Realizing the criticality of situation, I just grasped Tamanna's hand and strode towards the company's gate. I was almost tugging Tamanna along with me who kept on ranting all along the way.

His three friends hurried towards him who till then were gorging on the parathas and sniggering. I could see that he was still standing like a statue with one hand on his cheeks. He was aghast by the sudden change of events.

'Hey you, just stop there!' one of them hollered at us.

Our company campus was still at least 100 metres away so I speeded up but Tamanna kept on pulling me back. I didn't know why Tamanna was trying to be a superwoman who just a puff of air could easily thrash the goons. One tight slap was enough for her and at that point it was prudent to move towards the safe zone first. Nobody in the world can argue with the opposite sex, who always feel that whatever they do is right. It was extremely cold outside so even the guards were confined inside the guardroom.

In no time we were surrounded by the lecher and his three friends. My worst fear came true. I felt like slapping Tamanna for her obstinacy. Along with mine, she had also risked her own life.

The lecher who was fuming because of the humiliation he had to face screamed his lungs out.

'How dare you slap me? I will make you pay for this!'

He grasped Tamanna's hand and started pulling towards his car. Tamanna shrieked.

Now the lecher had crossed all limits and I had to react before it was too late.

'Leave her!' I yelled, holding her other hand firmly.

Unexpectedly, he took out his pistol and pointed it at me. I cringed.

'Let her go with us, otherwise…' he warned.

It was all beyond my imagination. My life was slowly getting back on track after the nightmare called the 'process party'. It had been only a week since I was duped by Radhika to befriend Tamanna once again and here I was anxiously standing at gunpoint just because Tamanna wanted to eat Chinese outside.

'Come on, God. I don't want to die like this. I am still a virgin,' I prayed.

'Are you leaving her or shall I shoot you?' he yelled, shuddering with anger.

All three of his friends and Tamanna stood there in complete shock.

'If something happens to her I won't ever be able to forgive myself. It's better to die than to let her go,' I thought.

Somehow I gathered courage and muttered, 'Sor…sorry, I can't.'

'You have to k…kill me,' I continued, even though I was scared to death. I just closed my eyes.

It all started near the Chinese van where Tamanna had unleashed her power on the face of one of the morons and all the hue and cry which followed after that made five or six *dhabawalas* come to our rescue. Soon a few others including cab drivers and employees encircled us. The *dhabawalas* were aware that if something bad happened it would put a full stop on their flourishing business. Nobody would be allowed to go outside after dark so they couldn't afford to let that happen. However the QRT who were ideally hired to provide protection and the company guards were conspicuous by their absence.

Seeing all this, the moron and his friends started to panic. Meanwhile I kept on holding her hand steadfastly as my confidence grew because of the overwhelming support from the *dhabawalas* and cab drivers minus the guards.

They realized that the tables had turned now and if they didn't act cautiously, the game would over for them. Even though it was cold outside we all were sweating as if it was the month of May, I, because a revolver was pointed at me. The hooligan leader was sweating because if he got caught then even God couldn't save him from the people standing there. Tamanna was stuck between the two of us.

'Let's move. The situation is bad now. We'll see them some other time,' one of his sidies whispered.

At that point of time I didn't know what his next step would be. He might fire at me or leave me. Meanwhile I kept on begging (I mean praying) God to save my life.

We all got to know of his decision soon enough. Suddenly he freed Tamanna from his grip and strode towards his car along with his friends and their car zipped out of the area. As far as I was concerned, it was a wise decision.

The entire episode took not more than five minutes, but those restless moments were the longest five minutes of my life. I was still in shock and didn't know how I pulled it off. It all looked so filmy till Tamanna turned and hugged me in front of all of them. Once again and as expected she started crying. I really don't know how females could produce so many tears. I think doctors need to re-examine the female body, whether it consists of 90 per cent water instead of 70 per cent which is the general perception. I too hugged her tightly and thanked God for saving my ass. In the meantime everyone present there started to clap. I felt a bit embarrassed but continued embracing her.

My life had come full circle within three months. A guy who had become the butt of jokes because of his misdeeds in the party had suddenly become an overnight celebrity in the company. Trust me, I was enjoying every bit of it. From the guards to the CEO everyone congratulated me for my bravery. However the company ensured to confine knowledge of the incident within the company's limits and advised the employees not to talk about the incident outside the premises as it might bring a bad name to the company. But it didn't affect my celebrity status at all. My life in the company had changed for good—or say excellent. Suddenly everyone wanted to be my friend including some snooty females including Deepika. I was sure that before all this they had hardly ever noticed me but post my death defying valour whenever our paths crossed, these pretty lasses would always pass smiles to me. Just the other day Prashant told me that Deepika had suddenly developed a liking for me and here was my golden chance to become her real boyfriend in the true sense.

The Chinese van had offered me a fifty per cent discount on all the items and also ensured that whenever I visited them my order would be served first, though it had become difficult to go out after that incident. Since that eventful day a police van had been positioned near the food area. I was skeptical whether the police would ever come to our rescue when actually required or would prove useless like the QRT. They were the last ones to reach the spot. I just hoped that it not happen again.

It was Prashant who had been benefited the most after I became a celebrity. He bragged about my bravery, and on top of it 'our friendship', among the girls. However Radhika remained the same. It seemed that for her an asshole remained an asshole.

But the most significant change was from Tamanna's side. She had already endured a lot in her relationship with Amit. It was just a matter of time before she would have ended her relationship with him. She needed an excuse and I think God had given her one. It was God's plan to send those four hooligans on that eventful day and ensure that I became her protector. By this God secured that Tamanna would eventually fall for me. Now I had taken Amit's place in her life. I mean, I had become her official boyfriend. Even though I could see Amit's missed calls and SMS on her mobile, she had discontinued answering them. Even though I was elated but somewhere I had a feeling that something was wrong.

Once again I could see flowers especially sunflowers blossoming around me. Sunflowers were her favourite flowers—and surprisingly she hated roses. It was a big bolt from the blue for me but when you talk about the opposite sex anything is possible. I could visualize myself running after Tamanna in a sunflower filled field. I knew it was an impact of watching too many romantic Bollywood movies but I loved it. I still don't know what the purpose of running was, but I kept on running after her. I guess only a movie director could answer that. Suddenly I started living a dream where everything from my professional to personal life was going smoothly.

Date Time with Tamanna

After Tamanna accepted me as her official boyfriend it was time to go for our very first date. Even though I was keen to invite Prashant and Radhika (I didn't know why) but Tamanna dissuaded me. She wanted it to be a private affair between me and her only. We planned to watch *Rab Ne Bana di Jodi* and then have dinner at Pizza Hut. Pizza Hut because she loved to gorge on Pizza Hut's pizzas only. For me all of them tasted the same.

I still remember my first movie and coincidently the only movie I had seen with my family was *Hum Aapke Hai Kaun* in a theatre way back in 1994. It had been over 14 years since that movie was released but that jig of Madhuri Dixit in the song '*Didi Tera Dewar Deewana*' still gives me goose bumps. Even though I was around 12 years old then I surreptitiously decided that someday I would marry Madhuri Dixit. Though that someday never came in my life and in 1999 my wish came to an abrupt end when she married

Dr Sriram Nene. I wept the whole day as if my world had been ransacked. Since then I had became a true movie buff though I ensured not to fall in love ever again with any other actress. I had seen umpteen movies including the morning ones either with my friends or at times alone. I never had the privilege of watching a movie with someone like Tamanna. It was not that I hadn't enjoyed watching all alone, in fact it helps you to concentrate more on the movie than to keep on passing popcorn and cold drinks. It's a different scenario where some people especially couples would pretend as if they were watching, but in reality busy doing their own stuff. I have named it the 'corner seat syndrome' because most of these things happen in and around corner seats only. These couples doesn't understand the effect they have on their co-audience who either get agitated or green-eyed.

I had booked the tickets for the 1 p/m/ show at PVR Saket. You would find people from all walks of life flocking there. Young couples with hands clutched together walking pointlessly, kids riding battery powered toy cars, jeeps which keep on bumping with people walking there. You would also find some people present there—especially unwanted singles—sitting on idly chairs and staring at females from every possible angle. This place was almost next to perfect for a date. Beside movies, there were plenty of options for eating out within the campus as it had umpteen numbers of eateries from Indian to Chinese on one side and from Pizza Hut to McDonalds on the other side. The only condition and an important one was that you needed to have money in your pocket otherwise this place would turn into a museum where you have the option to see things from outside but are not allowed to touch them. In case you couldn't afford to pay the bills, don't get disheartened, you still have the option of planning your date at the zoo economically and nature-friendly. Privacy is another add-on bonus there.

As planned I reached PVR Saket half an hour before the movie timings and waited for Tamanna. To surprise her, I even bought a bouquet for her. The florist charged almost triple the normal price. I believe that he had anticipated my excitement and thought that I could be his *bakra* of the day. I was sure he must be doing the same with other first-timer lovers like me. By now he must have become an expert in finding his daily *bakras*.

Soon, Tamanna arrived, wearing a yellow T-shirt and a black ruffled skirt. Her cute pink bag was hanging diagonally on her shoulder. As usual she was looking extremely cute. I don't know, but whenever I looked at her time froze for a few seconds. I believe it was an effect of watching too many romantic movies.

'Hi!' she smiled.

'Hello!' I replied, ensuring to hide the bouquet behind me.

'What you are trying to hide?' she enquired.

'N…nothing.' I hesitated. I didn't know why I was acting like an idiot.

'Show me,' she said, pointing her index finger at me.

'Got this for you,' I murmured as I handed over the bouquet to her.

'Thank you,' she chuckled. Her shining face compensated me for the extra amount that I'd paid to the florist.

'We still have 10 minutes before they allow entry,' I said.

'So…' she said, counting the number of flowers in the bouquet. As usual I was clueless. Maybe the number of flowers was directly proportional to how much one loves.

'We can roam around here,' I said.

'OK.'

We walked towards the McDonalds when suddenly a 7–8-year-old girl in a filthy dress pulled my T-shirt. She kept on repeating her parroted lines *'Jodi salamat rahe'* (May the couple live happily together).

The word *'jodi'* made me so elated that I decided to reward her with a 10-rupee note. But before I could pull my wallet out Tamanna stopped me.

'These street kids are very smart. They know how to make fools out of others,' she said.

Even an 8-year-old kid knew that I was an idiot, I thought!

'Whenever they see a couple they start begging for money. No need to give her any; she isn't disabled.'

Point to be noted: she was sensible.

'Let me show you something,' she said and turned towards the kid.

'Hey, will you work at my home? I will give you food, nice clothes, and after work you can watch television too,' Tamanna told her.

At first the kid didn't reply, but then she bluntly bawled, 'Go to hell!'

Within a few seconds she vanished from the scene. I don't know why she did that: if I had been in her place I'd have grabbed the opportunity with both hands. Free food plus free television was a deadly combination.

'See. This is the reality,' Tamanna said.

Still, I wanted to reward the poor kid for hailing us as a '*jodi*' but I couldn't.

'Poor girl! She met the right male but the wrong female,' I thought.

'You're right. Nobody wants to work, and begging is an easy profession,' I said.

The glow on her face clearly suggested how accurate her judgment about the kid was.

'Let's move. It's show time,' I said pointing to my watch.

It was a clumsy feeling to walk alongside her as I was not sure what others would be thinking of us as a pair. I and my friends used to make fun whenever we used to see any odd couples and our pairing could be easily defined as 'Beauty and the Beast'. Here, a mere kiss wouldn't transform a beast into a handsome prince. It only happens in a fictitious world and not in real life, where a frog remains a frog. Now the same thing was happening with me. It's wisely said that one should not make fun of others as you never know when you have to face a similar situation.

The security didn't allow us to take the bouquet inside. Even though we tried hard to persuade the security that it was just a bunch of flowers with no time bomb planted in it they were adamant. With no other options we had to relinquish the bouquet. My hard-earned money was dumped in the dustbin. Tamanna was crestfallen but it pained me even more when I came to know that we had the option of keeping the bouquet with the small shop located inside the premises for some petty charge but the security didn't share the same with us.

'Do you want anything?' I asked settling in my seat.

It was my first date so I had to behave like a gentleman. When you first fall in love, everything looks colourful around you. You ensure showing only your softer side howsoever irritating the situation may be. It's when you have spent some time that you begin to show your true colours.

'Yes, but only on one condition,' she replied.

'What?' I asked.

'I will pay for it.'

At first I couldn't believe what I heard. It's an unwritten law that when you are on a date all expenses would be borne by guys only. The only expectation from females is to relish the benefits.

Was she not aware of the basic principal? Then why was she not behaving like a typical Indian girlfriend?

'Come on, how can you pay?' I said. How could my male ego let a female pay for my snacks and that too on my first date?

'Then I won't have anything. You paid for the tickets; I will pay for the snacks. 50-50.' She smiled.

After a few seconds I gave in. My male self-esteem ran out of steam.

'OK,' I said.

I fetched two overpriced cold drinks and popcorn from the snack counter sponsored by Tamanna.

I had no interest in watching the movie. I just kept on staring her through the corner of my eyes. Her facial expression changed with every scene: if there was a comedy scene you could see her flashing her smile, if an emotional scene you could see her getting tense. I loved every moment of it. I was delighted to watch 'the movie with only one lead'

Tamanna than to watch the multi-starrer movie running in front of me.

The movie got over by 4 p.m. While getting out I felt a slight pain in my neck, probably because I'd kept watching her the whole time though it wasn't evident on my face.

As per the plan we headed towards Pizza Hut. But this time I ensured that I'd pay. Surprisingly this time she acted like a typical Indian girlfriend. We ordered medium-sized veggie supreme pizzas with coke.

'So how was the movie?' I asked.

'It was good but lengthy. By the way did you notice Anushka Sharma's earrings in that song? I wish I could get them,' she sighed.

Now who else apart from females could answer this. Only a female would notice, and given a chance make a note of what type of earrings or sandals the actress was wearing in each scene on a 70 mm screen. If you talk about guys the only thing that matters to them is how much cleavage the actress or vamp was showing on the screen, but to observe what kind of belt or shoes the actor was wearing is just absurd.

I just kept mum as I was not sure what to answer.

'It was too good, need to look out for that in Lajpat Nagar,' she answered herself.

'So did you inform you room partner about this?' I asked stirring the soup with the spoon.

'I just told them I was going out with my friend,' she winked.

'Oh OK,' I said.

'I used to do the same when I was with Amit,' she added.

The moment she took Amit's name, even though unintentionally, both my mood and soup spoon took a nosedive.

Do I have to spend the rest of my life being compared to her first boyfriend? I knew that she had stopped taking his calls but he was trying his best to woo her back. When she was with him he didn't realize her worth and now he wants her back in his life. Bastard!

Somehow she anticipated my feelings, and quickly changed the topic.

'So what's your hobby—apart from saving girls?' she smiled.

'Nothing much. I used to draw a lot when I was growing up,' I said with a straight face.

'I…I am sorry Shiv. I won't take his name again,' she whispered, pressing my palm.

Her gentle touch pulled my mood back to cloud nine.

'It's fine.'

'So why did you stop drawing?' she enquired while placing a slice of pizza on my plate.

'My dear this is India where every parent wants their child to become either an engineer, doctor or an IAS officer. It would definitely give a heart attack if any child discloses that he would like to be a painter,' I said.

'So I was never encouraged by my father and eventually I gave it up.'

'I understand.'

Again she pressed my palm and again I was elated.

The dinner was over and the bill was presented to me. That day I got to know why my friends, especially those who had girlfriends always nagged about money. Nowadays going on a date is an expensive affair.

Every good thing must come to an end, so it was time to say good bye. It was embarrassing to book an auto to drop her but I had no other option.

'How much for Malviya Nagar?' I asked the auto driver.

'Fifty rupees,' the auto driver replied firmly.

This is another problem area of being in love for the first few days. We have this mindset that if we start bargaining on our first date it would give a wrong impression. Even though I knew the idiot was charging an extra 20 rupees I still agreed as there was no point arguing with them.

It didn't take us long to reach Malviya Nagar and I decided to avail the same auto for my further journey.

'Just give me two minutes,' I requested the auto driver.

'OK, try to come fast,' he replied, ripping off a *gutka* sachet with his tobacco-stained teeth.

'Will do,' I smiled.

'So the day has come to an end,' I said dejectedly.

'Right, but don't worry, we'll meet on Monday,' Tamanna replied.

Though I was not expecting a good bye kiss from her but a formal hug would have been fine but that too didn't happen.

She walked towards her home and I turned towards the auto rickshaw. The auto driver kept on honking even though I promised to pay more than the actual fare.

All of a sudden I decided to turn back and yelled.

'Tamanna, one minute.'

She halted and turned towards me with a bewildered look.

I ran towards her and before she could apprehend anything I just pulled both her cheeks. Till this date I don't know what triggered me to do that.

'Let's go,' I said to the auto driver, gasping for breath. All this time I didn't turn back to check her reaction.

Instantly I got an SMS from Tamanna. 'Good night dear J'

Thank God! She liked what I did. I was relieved.

Not sure if she'd have reacted in a similar way if I'd kissed her. Content, I headed towards my locality.

My Coming of Age

'Hey guys, any plans for the extended weekend during Memorial Day?' Radhika asked.

'Nothing much, I think we shall go for a movie,' I said, looking at Tamanna.

'Hey, why don't we go to some nearby hill station?' Prashant pitched in.

'That's a nice idea,' Tamanna said gaily.

'But where?' I asked.

'Let's go to Nainital. It's a nice place to spend your weekend,' Prashant suggested.

'…and the best thing is that we can return in time before Tuesday evening,' he added.

'I'm in,' Radhika said merrily.

'Me too,' Tamanna voted.

When two people out of four, especially if they are females, decide upon something it would be next to impossible to counter that. For me Nainital or Mussoorie was one and the same thing so I hardly cared about the destination. All I was interested in was spending some quality time with Tamanna away from the office chaos.

After some time, at my workstation: 'I am dying to go to Nainital,' Prashant murmured.

'I think we all are. I had been to Mussoorie once when I was about 10 and I liked it a lot then. Nainital should be the same,' I replied.

'Radhika was right. An asshole would remain an asshole,' He said in irritation.

'Why, what happened?' I asked.

'Do you have any idea what's going to happen there?' he winked.

'What do you mean by "going to happen"?' I raised an eyebrow.

He replied with a wicked smile. I anticipated what he was trying to convey.

'You mean sex,' I whispered.

'Bingo!'

'Sshhhhhhhh. Control your emotions. Others are on call.' I patted on his back.

'Really, but I don't think it's good before marriage,' I continued. The reason I said so was because I grew up watching Shah Rukh Khan movies where a hero was expected to fall in love but not make love before marriage.

It seemed that Prashant went into coma after listening to what I just said. He was aghast.

'Hello…what happened?' I said snapping my fingers.

'Are you out of your mind? There's nothing wrong in that!' he said after recovering.

'It's the twenty-first century and love and sex are two sides of the same coin,' he preached.

'But both the sides are divided by a thin line called marriage, my friend,' I replied.

'There's no point in talking to you.' He shrugged.

'By the way have you ever done it?' I asked hesitantly.

'If you keep it to yourself only then will I disclose,' he said.

'Promise,' I assured him.

'Twice, and you know what, with different girls.' He winked.

'Are you serious?' I gaped. First I thought he was bragging but then I realized he never boasted about anything, not at least in front of me. He was not that sort of a person who would blabber about clearing an IAS examination but then out of the blue decides to work in a call centre.

Before I could ask anything he raised his right eyebrow and said. 'And you know one of them.'

'You mean Radhika?' I enquired my eyes popping out.

He just grinned.

'I…I mean, when?' I stammered.

'After I dropped you at your place when you were out of your senses,' he replied.

'Did you…?' I questioned again in disbelief.

'Of course we did. It just happened,' he replied confidently.

All of a sudden his Avaya blinked. It meant it was time to attend an incoming call.

'Will talk regarding this afterwards,' he said as he clicked the answering button.

'Thank you for calling…' he answered.

We were doing the graveyard shift so we needed to attend only a few calls.

Even in my wildest dream I never thought Radhika would be like that. Though it was her life and she was liberated enough to take her own decisions, but having been brought up in a conservative society it was hard for me to digest all that. It seemed having sex was not a big deal and that's why he used the term 'just happened'. I couldn't imagine something like that even though I was potent enough to be a porn star. I was not sure who fell in the pit that day, whether me or them, I thought.

My only intent was to spend quality time with Tamanna, and that's why I consented. It had been over four months since she started treating me as her boyfriend but not once did I touch her with any wrong intentions. Though Tamanna had started to talk about her periods lately, which I felt was a bit brave on her part, I always became nonplussed in such situations. Maybe it was an indication that she was ready for sex, still I was determined to not do anything before marriage.

Later that night I even discouraged Prashant's effort to talk about his sexual encounters and also made him vow that he would not do anything ethically 'wrong' in Nainital. The moment he heard my condition his face twisted in a grimace. His situation could be compared with that of a pizza delivery boy who is expected to carry pizzas all over the place and ensure timely delivery but he himself can't have a bite of it. Here, the pizza delivery boy was Prashant, and Radhika was the pizza.

At Anand Vihar Bus Terminal

I reached Anand Vihar Bus Terminal sharp at 9 p.m. The scheduled departure of our bus was 10 o'clock. The other three planned to reach together and I would join them at the bus terminal. My room was located closer to the Anand Vihar Bus Terminal as compared to them so I reached earlier and waited for them outside the main entrance. I was feeling a bit jittery and was hoping that everything went smoothly in Nainital.

Soon I could hear somebody hollering my name, 'Shiv, Shiv.'

It was Prashant (of course, who else) frantically calling my name. Radhika and the possessor of the cutest face in the world, Tamanna were following him.

'Hi Shiv,' he greeted and gave me a tight hug.

'Hello brother,' I replied, trying to release myself from his tight grip.

'So all set to go to Nainital?' he winked.

I apprehended what he meant but the moment he saw me scowling he changed tack.

'I…I was just joking, brother,' he grinned.

We all walked towards the terminal where our bus to Nainital was stationed. Once you become a boyfriend it's your duty to carry your girl's luggage irrespective of how heavy it is. The only thing she is entitled to carry is her handbag. Tamanna's luggage was so heavy, as if we were going on a months' tour and not on a two-day trip and the same with Radhika too. Though Prashant and Radhika had slept together only once and yet were not a couple officially, Prashant was hauling her baggage.

All of a sudden disaster struck when everything appeared to be in control.

While getting down a staircase Radhika somehow lost her balance and fell down.

'Oh God! Help!' she groaned.

Immediately Prashant got down on his knee and removed her shoes. The colour of her ankle turned red and soon inflated to almost double the size. It seemed she had twisted her ankle even though she was hardly carrying anything other than her mobile and her handbag.

'I guess the trip is over,' I sighed.

I was feeling bad for her but at the same time I was feeling extremely bad for myself as I could see the trip getting over even before it started.

'Can you walk?' Tamanna enquired.

The continuous trickling of tears down her cheeks clearly showed her excruciating condition. The obvious answer was no.

'What should we do now?' I asked.

'I can't go now! I need immediate medical assistance!' she was weeping continuously.

At times I feel pity for my own race. Whenever a pretty lass is in trouble everybody present around becomes overenthusiastic to help but when a guy is in a similar situation there's hardly anyone who cares. The same thing was happening at the moment: because of all the hue and cry courtesy Radhika, we were surrounded by onlookers and some of them even offered help.

'Let's cancel the trip and take her to a nearby hospital,' I said reluctantly.

Tamanna nodded in agreement.

'Wait. There's no point going back,' Prashant said solemnly.

Now he was acting crazy. Maybe the very thought of missing an opportunity to indulge in sex had made him talk rubbish.

'But, she can't walk!' I said.

'I can see that. But our money will go waste. We've booked two rooms there and now it's too late to cancel them,' he said.

'Right, but we don't have any other option,' I retorted.

In the meantime Radhika kept on crying and Tamanna was trying her best to console her.

'I have an idea. You both can go there and I can handle her,' He suggested, holding her lower leg.

I didn't respond, rather, looked at Tamanna, not sure what her response would be.

'At least you people can enjoy, we shall go next time,' he continued.

The moment Radhika heard his suggestion, the intensity of her crying doubled.

I wanted to give him a tight hug for the brilliant suggestion, but waited for Tamanna's response.

'A…are you comfortable?' I asked Tamanna.

She paused for a few seconds and then said, 'Let's go to Nainital.'

'She's quite a brave girl,' I thought.

We hired a taxi for the wailing Radhika and Prashant. After loading Radhika and her baggage in the taxi, it was time for a formal goodbye.

'You take care and keep me informed about her,' I said hugging him.

'Don't worry, I'm here to take care of her. You people enjoy the trip,' he responded. For the first time I realized that his feeling for Radhika was more than sex and felt proud of it. Once again it was proved that no one can go against his or her destiny. Just moments ago they were supposed to spend their weekend in the beautiful valley of Nainital but now they were forced to stay back.

'Tamanna, if you're not comfortable, you don't have to go,' I murmured.

'That's fine, Shiv; after all you are my boyfriend who saved my life,' she smiled, clutching my hand.

'Man, she really trusts me a lot!' I thought.

It took almost 10 hours to reach Nainital but I didn't complain. During the entire trip, she rested her head on my shoulder umpteen times and I ensured to remain still even though it did hurt like anything, but this is what you call sweet pain. It was a divine experience to see her sleeping and feel her breath. The best feeling was whenever she abruptly woke up with her eyes half closed due to a sudden jolt and I gently patted her to make her sleep again. It was truly holy.

We reached Nainital around 8 a.m. The weather was pleasant and it felt as if we were experiencing winter in the month of May. That's the beauty of a hill station like Nainital. There are only a few places in India where you actually feel like you're above the clouds and Nainital is one such place. Soon we reached our hotel located near the lake. We had booked two rooms at Nainital Dream Hotel. While filling up the customer information I noticed sceptical look on the receptionist's face even though I did inform him about the mishap of yesterday. He didn't utter a word but his facial expression made it evident that he thought us to be one of those young people who came there for only one thing, SEX.

We decided that we'd stay in separate rooms. Our hotel was situated at a height which gave a remarkable view of Naini Lake. One can spend the entire day just looking at the panoramic view of the lake. The whole view was just mesmerizing. Though the weather outside was pleasant we decided to visit the place in the evening as we were weary because of the journey.

We both rejuvenated after a bath and soon dozed off in our respective rooms.

(Knock, knock)

At first it felt like someone was banging on my head but I realized that someone was actually knocking at my door. With great difficulty I hauled myself to the door as I was still in the state of grogginess.

It was Tamanna.

'You're still sleeping! We're here to enjoy and not to sleep.' She scowled, entering the room.

'Ahh…' I replied absent-mindedly.

'Can we go out tomorrow? I'm really tired,' I pleaded.

To my surprise she agreed. Maybe she realized that I still needed three-four hours of sleep more to get back to normal.

'Only on one condition,' she said.

'W…what?' I asked.

'Come to my room at 9 o'clock sharp. We'll have dinner together in my room.'

I nodded.

'Now please let me sleep!' I pleaded. She smiled and left.

Once again I fell on my bed without realizing that post tonight my life would change forever.

(At 9'o clock)

'May I come in?' I asked.

'Come in. Just watching a repeat telecast of *Roadies* on MTV,' she said.

'Well, I'm really sorry for ruining your evening,' I said hesitantly.

'That's fine. We still have one day to roam around Nainital,' she said.

'The way you took care of me during the journey, you truly deserve extra rest,' she smiled.

I didn't know she'd noticed all the effort I had put in to make sure she was comfortable.

It was a double-bed room with attached bathroom, with wooden flooring and a 14"-inch TV in the corner which Tamanna was watching. The best thing I noticed in her room was a 'Do Not Disturb' sign which I didn't find in my room.

I sat on the other side of the bed keeping the maximum distance from her.

I don't know why, but I was feeling nervy sitting there. Even though we were couples for over four months but it was the first time we were all alone. It was raining mildly outside and the entire ambience around us was magical, but there was something fishy, and I wasn't aware of that.

'Do you want to order something?' I asked.

'No. Just order Coke for now.'

'OK,' I replied as I dialed room service.

'It'll take some time,' I informed her.

'For a Coke?' she asked.

I just shrugged.

She was hardly talking to me as she was engrossed in watching the TV show. I wasn't sure whether she was deliberately ignoring me or it was her favourite TV show.

She was looking breathtaking as usual, in a yellow T-shirt and short pants. The colour yellow complemented her beauty beyond words. I didn't expect or dream of spending time with such a beautiful girl in my life. I watched her through the corner of my eyes pretending that even I was keen to know who'd be the next MTV *Roadies* winner.

Suddenly I sensed that she was moving towards me inch by inch. Soon beads of sweats started to appear on my forehead. I swear by God that was a far worse situation than standing at gunpoint. Within two minutes I felt her hand touching mine. It felt like an electric shock as I quickly moved my hand away. That didn't cease her movements, as she continued to slide towards me and while doing that she kept looking at the TV.

'God, please help! What's she is trying to do?' I thought. Because of anxiety, I craved for water.

Inch by inch I moved towards the edge, reaching a the stage where I was balancing my entire weight on my left butt when somebody knocked at the door.

She quickly composed herself and returned to her original place. I heaved a sigh of relief.

'Thank God,' I muttered.

'I think your Coke is here,' I said, rushing to the door.

'Here is your Coke, Sir,' the attendant smiled.

'Thanks.'

He gave me a sly smile as I took the bottle from him. Maybe he was used to seeing people like us. I quickly handed over a 10-rupee note and shut the door even though I wanted it to remain open.

Once again we were on the bed watching TV, the only difference being that this time we were having Coke. She finished her's in a minute as if she was drinking water. Soon, as expected, the same scene was being repeated.

The moment she touched me again I was convinced she was doing it consciously. I decided that this time I wouldn't shy away even though I was sweating badly. My heart was beating faster and faster with every move by Tamanna.

Though I was trying my best to focus on the TV show, when your own life had become a reality show it was tough to focus on anything else. We had reached a moment where she was almost leaning on my body, but I remained motionless. I kept clutching the corner of the bedsheet.

Within seconds she turned her face towards me and kissed me on my lips. I don't have words to describe the feeling. I just closed my eyes. It was my first kiss on the lips from a girl aged more than 2 years. After watching my 'no response' for more than 10 agonizing minutes, she decided to act herself. She was convinced that if she didn't react right then she'd be sleeping all alone after dinner. Within minutes, she removed my T-shirt, and even though I wanted to touch her boobs I was reluctant to do so. But I didn't have to wait long: she grabbed my hands and started pressing them against her boobs. I could feel a lump in my throat. I didn't know how it happened, but the next thing I knew was that I was not a virgin anymore. It was something I lost, but still felt happy about. There are only a few things in life where even after losing them you actually feel proud about it, and this was one of them.

As expected we spent the entire next day in bed. I didn't know why the hell we came to Nainital and spent so much just to remain indoors.

'Will you marry me?' I asked, caressing her forehead. I had to abide by my philosophy of marriage.

She nodded in response and shed silent tears (as expected). I didn't know how to react other than to wipe off her tears.

Soon our trip ended and it was time to pack our bags and head back to Delhi. It was a trip where we paid the rent for two rooms but spent almost the entire trip in one room. We hardly visited any places in Nainital. In fact if you leave the pleasant weather and the hotel bills aside, it was hard to believe that we were on a trip. We'd even sacrificed our dinner for sex the previous night.

While making the final payment I observed the expression on the receptionist's face. I was sure he must be thinking that he hadn't ever seen despos like us. I was abashed by all this so refrained from making eye contact with him. While returning we kept on holding each other's hands and at times I even kissed her, ensuring our co-passengers didn't notice.

It was an unforgettable trip for me where I lost my virginity.

Guilt

It had been a week since we returned from Nainital but a lot had changed in my life, I'm not entirely sure whether for good or not. Losing your virginity and that too to someone you love was the best thing that could happen to someone, but along with happiness comes the sad part too. Somewhere I was feeling guilty of not adhering to my own 'Sex' philosophy. I always believed in having sex only after marriage, but here I'd done it consciously. Just a few days before the trip when Prashant had divulged his sexual encounter with Radhika I'd rebuked him and had even mentally degraded Radhika's character in no time. This guilt was killing me internally.

'So how was the trip?' Prashant grinned. He was dying to know what had happened between the two of us.

'It was OK,' I replied with a straight face.

'So did you do anything?' he smirked again.

Though I wanted to divulge the truth, somewhere I was afraid that he'd stop taking me seriously after getting aware of the truth.

'No…nothing. We stayed in our separate rooms only,' I said timidly.

'Really!' He raised his eyebrow.

'Y…yes. Don't you trust my word?' I said, avoiding making eye contact with him.

'As expected. You got a golden chance and you missed that. Terrible.' He sighed.

I didn't reply and acted as if I was checking my emails. I didn't want to continue the topic as he was too smart to pinpoint the loopholes and catch me red-handed.

I was not sure of Tamanna's current state of mind but was dying to talk to someone sensible about my guilt. It was impractical to talk to Prashant about this, and the only other person left was Radhika. The only apprehension was how to approach her.

'Hey, how's your ankle?' I enquired, looking at her swollen ankle.

'It's getting better day by day but the doc advised me not to put pressure on it,' she replied.

'That's good,' I said.

'This reminds me of something. Did you get time to visit Mukteshwar?' she enquired.

'Actually…' I pursed my lips.

'What, Shiv? Was everything fine in Nainital?' She enquired.

'Ya…it was good, but…' I mumbled.

She immediately sensed that something was bothering me.

'But what?' she coaxed.

'I don't know how to talk about all this,' I expressed my discomfort.

'It's fine. You can share it with me,' she said pressing my left shoulder.

Though age wise she was younger than me but maturity wise she could easily be my grandmother.

'Ac...actually something happened in Nainital which shouldn't have happened,' I hesitated.

Due to embarrassment, I avoided eye contact with her.

'You mean hankie pinkie?' she whispered.

'Y...yes,' I muttered. I was still looking at the floor.

'Really. I'm impressed!' She chuckled.

'Easy, Radhika. Others may hear,' I cautioned.

'Oh OK. So what's the problem?' she asked.

'I'm feeling guilty,' I said looking elsewhere while talking to her.

'For God's sake stop wasting your time thinking about it. It's the twenty-first century and you have not done anything wrong. It happens,' she said.

I kept mum.

'Come on, you haven't betrayed her, and it was not a mere one-night stand between the two of you. You genuinely love her, and just think, if I wouldn't have hurt my ankle that day I'm sure nothing like this would've happened. Am I not *right*?' she asked, stressing the word right.

'Right,' I replied after a few seconds.

'It was all destiny so for God's sake stop blaming yourself.'

She was right: if she hadn't hurt her ankle we all would've been in Nainital and I wouldn't have done something like that. Somewhere down I knew my intention was to spend some quality time with Tamanna and not to indulge in hanky panky in Nainital. Also, I loved Tamanna like crazy, so unless she changed her mind at the last moment, I would definitely marry her. I never considered all the relevant points made by Radhika earlier. Finally, I was relieved. Once again it was Radhika who pacified me.

We'd already demolished the last wall standing between the two of us, the great wall of Virginity. She stayed with her room partner on the third floor in Malviya Nagar. Occasionally I started boarding her cab or some other cab on her route to visit her. The only instruction was to climb the stairs slowly and sturdily and ensure nobody was watching, especially her landlord. The kind of graveyard shifts the call centre employees have to do, it was unlikely to be caught red-handed by her, or even any landlord in the middle of the night.

Her flat consisted of two rooms, one large room almost double the size of my entire flat in Shakarpur and another room, smaller, but with the benefit of fitted wooden cupboards. Just adjacent to her building there was an open park, exactly the opposite of my congested locality in Shakarpur where experiencing direct sunlight and that too in your room was a luxury limited to the few Ambanis and Tatas of our locality. Maybe that was one difference between the two flats, and it was clearly evident by the rent charged by the landlords in these localities.

'Hi,' I said the moment she opened the door.

'Shhhh. Easy, the neighbour might hear us,' she replied.

I immediately stepped inside her room. Her room partner had already left for her morning shift. Everything was well arranged in her room. It really proved that one needs to have a female to create a home out of a room. I was invited to taste her favourite dish, *pulao*, cooking which she told me she was an expert at.

My eyes roved around to inspect the room, filled with fur toys especially teddy bears of all sizes one could imagine. Just by counting the number of teddy bears in a girl's room one could estimate how many affairs she'd had till date, especially if she was over 16.

In that sense, Tamanna could easily surpass 90 per cent of the girl's population.

Even though I'd slept with her once, I was still feeling hesitant at embracing her.

I guess it would take some more time to get used to all that.

She got two cups of coffee from the kitchen.

'So how is my room?' she enquired, blowing at her coffee to cool it.

'It's nice, but so many fur toys…' I commented.

'Oh yes. These are gifted by Amit,' she said.

My worst fears came true the moment she took Amit's name. Within seconds the cute looking teddy bear got transformed into a real-life bear with overgrown fangs and long nails who seemed to be dying for my blood at that moment.

'OK. Anyways did you talk to Radhika about Nainital?' I asked trying to divert my attention from the teddy bears. I wanted to know whether she too had a guilty conscience or not.

'Nothing much, except that we kissed each other,' she smiled.

'Really!' I said raising my left eyebrow.

'Relax, Shiv. Do you really think I'd share my personal experiences with someone whom I know only on a professional level?' she said.

'No. Never,' she declared.

'Is there a problem in sharing your secrets?' I asked.

'Shiv, it's not that I don't trust her, but there are things in life which you need to keep to yourself only. It's too personal,' she explained.

'If tomorrow Radhika divulges the truth, I'd definitely be a dead man,' I thought.

'How on Earth could I be so irresponsible? But then I didn't have any other option. I was dying with the guilt,' I pondered.

I just hoped Radhika kept her promise of not sharing my secrets with anyone else in the office, especially with Prashant.

Once again we both were all alone, this time not in Nainital but in her room in Malviya Nagar. I really felt like kissing her, but the very thought of slipping back into another episode of guilt halted me.

She got busy preparing *pulao*. I joined her in the kitchen. After much reluctance she allowed me to peel the peas for her *pulao*.

I had never ever assisted Rohit in the kitchen and here I was wholeheartedly peeling peas for Tamanna. That's what a women's presence can do in your life. I was really feeling bad for Rohit who till date prepared food for me without uttering a word whenever our maid was on leave.

'You know what?' Tamanna said, igniting the burner to place the cooker on it.

'What?' I asked.

'It's about your appreciation email from Tushar,' she said.

'Thank God! For the first time I've got appreciation for my work,' I smiled.

'But somewhere I felt that Radhika didn't like it,' she said, pouring freshly cut slices of onions in the cooker, producing a hissing sound.

'Come on. She's a friend. Why should she feel insecure about my appreciation?' I asked.

'It's just that I heard from someone she talked to about your appreciation email from Tushar. According to her you didn't do anything exceptional and there was no need for such appreciation,' she replied, stirring the onions in the cooker. The aroma of frying onions filled the environment around us.

'You girls will remain girls. Did you hear her saying that?' I asked.

'Nope, but I think she's not comfortable with your sudden rise in status,' she said.

'...and don't forget she's due for promotion soon,' she said apprehensively.

'Yaa, I know. But I don't think I'd hamper her chances in any way,' I said.

'Right, but you saved the company's reputation, which she didn't. It might create problema for her,' she said.

'Do you really think so?' I asked.

'Might be.'

'Don't you think you're taking it a bit too seriously'?

'I don't know. I just want you to be prepared beforehand.' she smiled.

You can't have smoke without fire. Was there something fishy which I should be worried about? The last thing I wanted was to lose a friend and mentor like Radhika.

We returned to the room after half an hour in the kitchen preparing *pulao*.

I didn't know what encouraged her to kiss me the moment we slumped on her bed. Kissing was really intoxicating. I almost lost my senses but the cooker's untimely whistle brought us back to the real world. We both started laughing.

Friendship vs Promotion

At last life had started to show some consideration for me both personally and professionally. I had the best girlfriend one could imagine considering my ordinary job and equally ordinary looks. The valor I showed in protecting her from hooligans did wonders to my self-confidence. It was eventually showing in my calls too. I was getting better with each passing week. At times I felt like thanking those lechers for bringing out the best in me otherwise I'd have remained timid all my life. I was doing the same shift as Radhika's. Tamanna and Prashant were doing shifts two hours later than mine. Even though I had the privilege of choosing my own shift I desisted from doing that.

'You know what? I've heard something,' Radhika said, adjusting her headphone.

'What?' I replied while going through my emails.

'You'll soon be getting a promotion.'

'Are you serious?' I paused, looking at her.

'Yes. After all, you saved a girl,' she said. I ignored the sarcasm.

'Come on, do you really believe all these rumors?' I tried to be casual.

'This news is confirmed. Sanjay told us,'she said.

'But how can you trust Sanjay? He's not at all reliable.'

'Man, you're overlooking something. He's on good terms with Sandeep, our Senior Manager who himself informed him about this latest development,' she said.

I knew the reason behind the cordial relationship between Sanjay and Sandeep. Even though Sandeep was on the wrong side of 30 he was still a bachelor. I had heard that Sanjay at times arranged call girls for him, usually on weekends. Not sure whether higher management was aware of his wrong deeds, but because of his flawless work he was untouched till date. He even befriended female employees and exploited them sexually. I'd even heard that he got one of our ex-employees pregnant and later forced her to go for an abortion. Not sure how much truth there was in that particular case as it happened way before we joined the company. So if Sandeep had enlightened about my promotion it could not be dismissed so lightly.

'Along with Tamanna, you also safeguarded the company's reputation as well. It may happen as early as next week,' she continued.

At first the unexpected news of my promotion made me elated. By no means was it a mean feat considering it was not even a year since I joined the company. It was like securing the first rank in the UPSC exam in your first attempt. People spent year after year in a BPO or in any private organization before they got any promotion. It's irrelevant how well deserving you are as a candidate, unless you've licked your boss' ass you can't imagine yourself being promoted. I'm sure not more than 10 per cent promotions are legitimate.

But once my emotions calmed down, I perceived the true picture behind my promotion. It was my pluck and not my work which was doing all that. Radhika was almost four years older in the system and was an awesome caller since day one. Till date nobody scored more perfect Bulls Eye calls than her. She had even sacrificed her holidays just to be in office. When half of India was busy lighting up small clay lamps and candles around their houses during Diwali, she willingly decided to enlighten an irate customer over a call.

Fuck. I will never do that.

She once told me that she wanted to move up the ladder in the BPO sector only. She joined ('plunged into', to be precise) the BPO industry at a very young age due to her modest financial condition. Her childhood dream was to become a fashion designer like Ritu Beri but her financial situation had planned something else for her. She was serious about her job and that's why she was always willing to work on holidays as well. It was her conviction that one day the company would recognize her hard work and reward her accordingly in the form of promotion. Somewhere I believe that losing on her dream of becoming a fashion designer had made her even more determined. Unfortunately she was relying heavily on her hard work and overlooking an important aspect called destiny. In the past it was her destiny which didn't let her pursue her dream, and once again it was playing spoilsport. We all were sure that she'd be the first choice for any elevation in the process but my fortuitous bravery had ruined her chances. I never dreamt that one day I'd have to vie with my own friend even though I didn't ask for it. A rift had developed between us, and it started to show up. Was this the beginning of the end of our friendship? Would Tamanna's prediction come true? Only time would tell.

I made myself available for calls, but her sarcasm perturbed me thoroughly. Is professional friendship just a myth and not a reality? I mean, if one gets promotion early, is it necessary that the other would feel dejected at the same time? I was very aware of the fact that if my bravery was kept aside I'd be the last person to be considered for any kind of promotion. The management wanted to reward me for my actions and not my work. I too yearn for promotions just like any other employee, but certainly not at the cost of losing my friend.

'Hey Mama! Where are you?' SMS from Tamanna.

Yes, she'd started addressing me as 'Mama' and I was getting used to it. I guess referring your to boyfriend with familiar names like Mama, Papa, etc. makes you feel more connected.

'I'm in office, Mama *ka beta*,' I replied.

'See you in 10 minutesJ' from Tamanna.

After Some Time

'...I didn't do it for promotion. You know that,' I wrote to Tamanna on SameTime. I informed her what had transpired between me and Radhika moments ago, especially her acerbic tone.

'See. I warned you,' she replied.

'I know, but what if that asshole had opened fire? I'd have died then,' I keyed in.

'Chill, Shiv,' she replied. Calling me by my real name meant that she was livid now.

Before I could write anything further she continued.

'Shiv, you know her well and her past. I'm sure if you had been in her place you too would have been miffed with what's happening.'

'I know that. In fact I'd have definitely gone mad but...' I wrote.

'But what?'

'But Radhika needs to understand this. It's not my fault that I'm being considered for promotion: it's management which takes the decision. She should not talk to me like this,' I wrote.

'You need to give her time. The wound (news of your promotion) is fresh; it would take some time to heal]' she wrote.

'I think you're right. I just hope so...' I wrote.

'...but I am elated now,' she wrote.

'Why?' I enquired.

'My boyfriend is about to become a Team Leader. At least now I can introduce you to my parents!'

'Hmmmm,' I wrote.

'...but nothing is concrete now: it's just a rumour,' I continued.

In today's world your position matters the most. Furthermore, you can't afford to fall in love on an empty stomach.

With each passing day, the crack was getting wider and wider. Radhika had stopped going on breaks with us especially when I was around. Earlier she used to assist in every possible way. In fact I still remember that once she deliberately disconnected her own call just to help me out. But these days even after repeated requests she hardly responded. Just the other day she even chided me for no fault of mine. Though I didn't react, her uncanny behaviour was killing me. Even though Prashant was normal I was sure that sooner or later he too would join her.

'Is it the same with childhood friends too? What about SRK? Do his classmates too feel the same way Radhika is feeling right now?' Weird thoughts like that kept passing through my mind.

One Week Later

'Best of luck for your interview, Mama!' Tamanna chuckled on the phone.

She knew that Tushar had set up a meeting to discuss my promotion and most probably I'd be getting my letters that day itself.

'Thanks, dear.'

'Don't worry about Radhika. She'll be fine,' she replied. I just kept mum.

'Just concentrate on your interview,' she advised.

I was feeling gloomy on one of the most important days of my professional career. On one hand, my Associate tag would be getting replaced by a Team Leader tag while on the other hand I was on the verge of losing one of my best friends, Radhika. Almost everyone wished me good luck even though half-heartedly but Radhika out rightly ignored me.

In Tushars' Cabin

'May I come in, Sir?' I said as I knocked at the door.

'Yes, Shiv,' he said, perking up.

'Have a seat. Need to talk to you something important,' he smiled.

He was looking dashing as usual. I still couldn't believe that he was squandering his good looks in this small cabin while he could easily act in movies.

'I have an important announcement to make,' he said.

I didn't utter a word and just nodded.

'Shiv, by protecting a female colleague of yours, you have not only shown singular courage but also leadership qualities. You have proven that in time of need, you will stand and face the challenge rather than run from it. As per Varun, your scores are getting better each week. Taking all this into consideration, the management has decided to promote you as a Team Leader.' His face broke into a broad smile.

He must have anticipated that on hearing that I'd break into a jig but I kept quiet.

'Shiv, is everything all right? Are you not happy with this?' he enquired, seeing my deadpan reaction.

'No…no Sir. It's nothing like that. I am honoured that management has thought about me, but I want to say something if you permit,' I said hesitantly.

'Sure, Shiv.'

'What if I wasn't present that day? Would the management have thought the same as it does now?' I murmured.

Now it was Tushar's turn to keep mum.

'I did what I thought was right then, but somewhere my conscience is not allowing me to accept this promotion just because I the saved company's reputation,' I said.

One should have seen Tushar's face. He was shell-shocked and didn't know how to react.

'There are many who are older and better performers than me. It would give a wrong message to all of them,' I said.

I didn't know why I was digging my own grave. If Tamanna got to know, she'd definitely kill me.

'People like Radhika who had worked really hard and did almost everything possible on Earth for the next promotion would feel let down by this step,' I continued.

Tushar kept listening.

'Her four years of hardship would go in vain if I get the promotion,' I wound up.

'I understand what you mean, Shiv, but these decisions are being made by higher management and not me,' he said.

'I know, Sir,' I replied, pursing my lips.

'OK. So what do you want now?' he questioned.

'To be honest, I don't know, Sir. Maybe I want to spend some more time in the company before I could accept something like this,' I said.

'OK Shiv, as you wish. Now I really need to think what I should say to the higher management,' he sighed.

'Maybe that I need some grooming before I am considered for the next promotion?' I said.

'Hmmm.'

'If you don't mind may I ask you something?' he said.

'Sure Sir,' I replied.

'I hope you know what you are doing. It's a once-in-a-lifetime opportunity and you never know when it would happen the next time. It might not ever happen,' he warned.

'Yes Sir,' I smiled.

Now who would tell him that even I was not sure why I did that. The only thing I was like slapping myself for cutting my own nose to spite my face.

'…and one humble request Sir. Whatever transpired between you and me must remain secret,' I requested.

'Don't worry,' he replied.

As I moved towards the door he called me.

'Shiv, I will assign some reports to you. Going forward I want you to work on them. I hope you are good in Excel,' he said.

'Sure Sir. I'll try my best,' I replied and turned to the door.

'And one more thing. My decision to fight for you with HR after the party has proven right today.'. He smiled and got busy on his laptop.

When your boss appreciates you it really means a lot when you know it's genuine admiration. I was content when I left the room.

It seemed that almost everybody wanted to know what happened behind the closed doors. The moment I returned to my desk everybody congregated around me. I knew except for Tamanna (because she was my girlfriend) and Prashant (who was not seeking any future in the organization) everybody else would be delighted to know that I didn't get any promotion but would still sympathize with me.

'What happened?' Ashok asked digging his nose as usual.

I didn't reply and made a gloomy face instead. I acted as if somebody had stabbed me in my back.

'Is everything all right? What did Tushar say?' Tamanna enquired. She looked concerned.

'N…nothing much, except he wants me to work on a few Excel reports,' I murmured.

'And what about promotion?' she asked me again.

'He…didn't talk about it,' I grumbled.

'What!' she almost yelled. She couldn't believe what I'd just said. Her plan of getting me introduced to her parents as a Team Leader had gone for a toss. I doubt whether her parents—or say any girl's parents—would be interested in meeting a prospective bridegroom who was just an associate in a BPO.

'I'll kill that wimp,' Prashant ranted, referring to Sanjay who divulged the news first. Coincidently he was on leave for that entire week so he was safe.

'Even I want to,' I said angrily. I was faking to ensure that everybody around me especially Tamanna would feel that I was deeply hurt by the turn of events.

The news of my failure reinvigorated my so-called colleagues in the process especially the veterans in the process including Radhika. I could hear a few sniggers but decided to disregard them.

'Don't worry, brother. Everything will be alright,' Ashok whispered, patting my shoulder.

Even though it was genuine empathy I didn't like his touch for obvious reasons.

Somebody has truly said that whatever you do you can't make everyone happy. The same thing was happening with me. Radhika was back on talking terms with me, but at the same time Tamanna was agitated. She didn't talk about my promotion after that day but ensured to show her desperation through her behaviour. I never thought that my promotion meant so much for her otherwise I'd have accepted Tushar's offer. It's palpable that most of us would choose love over friendship and I was no exception. I just hoped to get everything back to normal between me and Tamanna. At times I thought life was much easier before I met these two females.

Even though Tamanna was agitated with me but somewhere I knew I did the right thing by not accepting the promotion.

Jack of All Trades

It had been almost two months but nothing had changed much for me, instead things were getting murkier with each passing day. Even though my promotion had been postponed indefinitely I was still not able to bridge the gap between me and Radhika. Though she started talking to me but it was nothing like it used to be before Sanjay spilled the beans about my promotion. Not only had I lost my golden opportunity of getting elevation in the company but also my friend Radhika. And on top of it by doing all, I had made Tamanna cranky.

It might be a coincidence but after that day my comparison with Amit had suddenly increased. His dressing style, his favourite brands, his sense of humour blah blah and more blah. The only thing left for comparison was my underwear brand. At the beginning I was taking it flippantly but with each passing day my life was becoming more and more thorny. I didn't know what to do next. My problem was that I never had the privilege of falling in love in the past and that too with a girl who had been in a relationship for quite some time.

There was no point apprising her of the truth. It would only add to my existing suffering. Radhika had ensured that apart from process related queries she would pretend checking her already checked emails. With Sanjay, if you talked anything apart from sex he'd be least concerned. Only yesterday he was talking about Deepika. He wanted me to tempt Deepika to his residence for a weekend party but I rejected it knowing his libidinous intentions.

In between the management had introduced a contest named Jack of All Trades which would run for three months and whoever scored the highest marks on several parameters would be awarded handsomely. For now it was a secret for all of us. As per management there were only a few parameters but in reality it included everything under the sun including how much time you had spent in the washroom. From your leaves to your weekly scores, how much time you were present on the call to how much sale you would achieve and the list went on.

We all had assembled in the meeting room to get the standings at the end of the second month.

'Hello everyone,' Varun greeted us.

'I know you all are working hard for the Jack of All Trades contest. But now it's time to further tighten your belts as only a month is left,' he announced.

I was least interested in his spirited speech. I was losing my sleep over the plan cancelled by Tamanna early in the day. It had been over two months since I last kissed her and I was dying to spend some quality time with her but she was not letting me do that. Because of Radhika my sex life had also dried up. I wished I could go back in time and reverse my preposterousness. Considering everything, I should have accepted Tushar's proposal.

'Shiv has shown tremendous improvement and has moved to third spot. Tamanna is still on second spot, headed by Radhika. So everyone please clap for Radhika,' he declared.

Everyone present started to clap. One should have seen Radhika's face which was gleaming at the moment with pride. I didn't know about others, but for me she truly deserved all the accolades.

I was working my ass off to improve my scores but it was frustrating to know from Prashant that a few in the team were linking it to my proximity with the management, especially with Tushar. The blessing was turning into a curse. Everyone around me whether Tamanna, Radhika or my colleagues had some issue with me. I didn't care a fuck for my teammates but Tamanna and Radhika were two of the most important people in my life, and I was dying to resolve the differences between us.

The only person with whom I could talk at the moment was Prashant.

'Hi Prashant. Can we go for a sutta break? Need to talk something important,' I wrote on ST.

'What happened?' he asked.

'Well, it's about Radhika. Please don't take it otherwise...' I wrote.

'It's OK, buddy. You are my friend first, so go ahead,' he wrote.

I was hesitant to write about the weird behaviour of Radhika but his words alleviated me. It's really tough to find someone who would give preference to friendship over love. I am sure a few would disagree, but when I attach love with sex then most of you would concur.

'I have noticed that Radhika's behaviour has changed a lot. Is there a problem?' I wrote.

'Let's go out. Will talk there,' he suggested.

'OK.'

Soon we both were standing in the middle of avid smokers in the smoking area. At times it was impossible to make out someone inside the smoking area from a distance due to continuous emission of smoke by these smokers. I craved to know the reason why they smoked so much. Once Prashant told me that it unwound them. Maybe he was right, but to be honest I had never seen a person whose life had been benefited by smoking. You talk of any disease irrespective of which part of the world you live in or which race you belong to and you will find smoking as one of the causes behind that disease. Unfortunately smoking is not racist: it treats everyone the same. I really feel pity for people who even though theoretically educated but practically act as an illiterate who can't even read the statutory warning clearly mentioned on every packet that 'Smoking is injurious to health'.

I did my best to stop Prashant from smoking but he always overlooked my advice. The only thing he did as a token of concern was to reduce his daily intake of almost a packet to two-three cigarettes. I just hoped that one day he would liberate himself from smoking.

'You're right, Shiv. To be honest she couldn't digest the fact that a guy who was hired after her and that too because of one incident was hogging all the limelight in terms of promotion,' He said, blowing smoke rings. Man, he'd become an expert in blowing almost perfect smoke rings.

'You know that she was expecting a growth this time. But your ill-timed fame killed her chances,' he sighed, stubbing the cigarette on the ground.

'You know what? She even missed Diwali just to be on call,' he said lighting up another cigarette.

I didn't utter a word as it was his second cigarette of the day. I was waiting to see whether he'd light up yet another one or not.

'Idiot. She only missed her Diwali. Here, I not only lost a golden opportunity to grow but also had to face Tamanna's wrath,' I thought.

'I know, Prashant. Even I am not happy. I never want to grow at someone else's expense, leave alone Radhika. I really don't want to lose a friend like her. I really don't know what to do,' I said in my helplessness.

'I know, brother. She always changes the topic whenever I try to talk about you.' He shrugged.

'This reminds me of something, Shiv. I want to ask something.'

'What?'

'How come you didn't get your promotion letter? I did talk to Sanjay and he swore by his daughter that Sandeep told him about your promotion,' he asked, raising his eyebrow.

'I…I don't know, Prashant,' I replied hesitantly. Sweat beads appeared on my forehead.

'Are you trying to hide something?' he interrogated.

'Why…why would I? Tushar might have changed his decision at the last moment,' I stammered.

'Let's move in, it's getting time. We need to make ourselves available on call,' I said, staring at my watch.

'O…OK. Let me finish my cigarette.'

He didn't pose any further question but I doubt he believed what I said.

We all worked like asses to climb up the ladder for the Jack of All Trades contest. Just to secure the maximum marks and the first position I even cut down on my pee breaks. If I could secure first position, I could win Tamanna's heart once again. So I wanted to give my 200 per cent. I knew if I had to conquer 'The Great Wall of Radhika' I had to give in everything I possessed for the next one month. In order to score more marks I even extended my shifts on a few days unlike Radhika. Surprisingly Radhika didn't extend her shift even once, especially during the last one month. That was a mystery and I didn't have time to resolve it. In reality it was bridging the gap between the two of us on the ranking chart. I was more worried on how to win back my love and the only way was by securing the first rank in the competition.

Soon the result day arrived. Everyone on the floor was asked to assemble in the breakout area. Tushar would be announcing the winner of the Jack of All Trades competition and the 'surprise' prize. I was still skeptical whether I had done enough to score the first rank or not. I wished I had a few extra days to work just to be on the safe side but then it would have been a biased contest. I just prayed and slowly slogged towards the breakout area.

One could hear whispers all around when Tushar made his entry in the breakout area.

'First of all I would like to congratulate you all for your relentless efforts which you have put in to make the contest a great success. So give yourself a great round of applause,' he announced and started to clap and soon everyone followed him.

In the meantime I was busy making all possible calculations in my mind.

Tamanna took three days leaves during the contest so she was not going to make it. On the other hand Prashant was not at all serious about the competition from day one so one could count him out. Again, it narrowed the competition to between Radhika and me. This time I was frantic to win even though it meant losing my friend Radhika. I knew that this time I really worked hard and was not dependent on my luck to be declared the winner.

But the question was, 'Did I work enough to surpass someone like Radhika?' I thought.

'…so the winner of the Jack of All Trades is…' he tore open the envelop to pull out the winner's name.

Meanwhile my heart started pounding really hard and fast. My hands started trembling due to anxiety.

'Any guesses guys?' he smiled.

'Come on, stop it. Here I was dying and he wanted people to guess. Just finish it off otherwise I'd die of a heart attack,' I thought.

I don't know why in moments like these the announcers like people to make a guess without realizing the effect it creates in the hearts of the nominees.

'Radhika!' somebody yelled, echoed by Prashant.

Nobody took my name as expected. Even Tamanna decided to keep mum.

'Sorry guys. The winner of Jack of All Trades is Shiv!' Tushar declared.

I was busy praying with my eyes shut when Tushar announced my name. It felt like being in heaven. It almost felt the same when I lost my virginity in Nianital. Sex and success goes hand in hand, I thought.

Almost everybody gathered around me and started congratulating me for my victory. Somebody muttered that it was all fixed. Though I wanted to punch him I somehow managed to control my emotions.

'…and the prize for winning the Jack of All Trades is vouchers worth 10,000!' Tushar further announced.

'Come here, Shiv and collect your vouchers,' he said.

I slowly walked towards him. He shook hands with me and handed an envelope with vouchers in it.

'Congratulations!' he said.

'Thank you, Sir,' I replied. Everyone continued to clap.

We both posed for a photograph which would be emailed to all the associates in the company. Soon after everyone returned to their workstations.

Tamanna was delighted and congratulated me. She shook hands with me even though she wanted to hug me. That's what I presumed by her gesture.

Prashant hugged me as usual and lifted me. 'So proud of you, brother!' he shouted.

'Thanks, brother, but Radhika…' I said.

'Don't worry, she'll be fine,' he winked. I didn't get what he meant by that when suddenly Deepika appeared in front of me.

'Congrats, Shiv. So when is the party?' she said in her flirtatious tone and before I could realize she hugged me. She was flirting big time with me.

I could feel her boobs pressing against my chest and I knew it was deliberate. I felt embarrassed but she looked OK as if nothing had happened. She continued to give her sensuous smile. I didn't know how I composed myself and uttered 'Tha…thanks, Deep…ika,' I mumbled.

Not sure whether it was an indirect invitation to go out and eat with her. No doubt she was too hot, but somehow my SRK-type love philosophy of spending my life with one woman stopped me from a further reply. My love philosophy was ruining my sex life, I thought.

Only a guy can realize what it feels like getting a hug from a sexy lass, and even tougher not to reciprocate because you are already committed to someone else.

I could see Sanjay's eyes popping out from their sockets. I just wished that Tamanna missed what Deepika did otherwise I could be dead. Girls don't see others' faults, they just hold you responsible for deeds like these so I needed to be careful.

The first thing after you win any cash reward is to sum up the total amount of the vouchers whether it's adding up to what it had been promised or not so that any deviation on the lesser side could be reported to the management. I too started counting my vouchers when I saw an ST message from Radhika.

'Hi Shiv, Congratulations!' she wrote.

It was a big surprise for me as I wasn't expecting her to congratulate me.

'Thanks dear, it means a lot to me,' I wrote back.

'May I come to your workstation for a moment?' she asked. In order to keep a safe distance from me she'd even changed her workstation.

'One thing, Shiv. I want to say s…sorry,' she mumbled.

'Sorry? For what?' I acted as if nothing happened.

'For intentionally ignoring you,' she almost blubbered.

'I had become selfish without realizing you didn't do it personally,' she continued.

Tears were pouring down her face showing her genuine remorse. I was taken aback by her sudden change of tune. I didn't react at all, instead I offered my handkerchief to wipe her tears. It's well said when a girl is crying it's best to let her finish because if you dare to interrupt in the middle it would add fuel to the fire.

I didn't know what made a devil suddenly act like a saint, and that too after the devil had just lost a battle.

'Because of me you withdrew your promotion,' she exploded the bomb. Now she was crying badly. Almost everybody turned to look at us.

Tamanna was on call so she couldn't rush and Prashant was out on his sutta break.

'Hey, it's OK dear. Nothing like that happened.' I tried to pacify her.

'Don't lie. Prashant told me,' she said, wailing like a 2-year-old toddler.

'What?' I yelled. I was flabbergasted as how Prashant had came to know about what transpired between me and Tushar behind closed doors.

'It's OK and for God's sake please keep your voice low. If Tamanna gets to know all this she'll kill me!' I pleaded, looking at Tamanna who was still engaged in her call.

'OK. OK, but you have to forgive me,' she said, lowering her voice. Only females can make an apology feel like a threat.

'Yes, my dear. I'm happy that you realized that it was not my mistake. It was all destiny,' I said.

'You are my friend and if something is bothering you, do share it with me. There is cut-throat completion to move up the ladder, unlike school, but I can expect transparency from a few, including you. I really don't want to lose my friend,' I said.

'Thanks once again,' she said cheerily and gave me a friendly hug. There is a huge difference between a deliberate hug and a friendly hug, though for some people, especially those like Sanjay, it was all the same. Suddenly her red cheeks turned back to normal.

'It's done and dusted. Forget everything; let's start afresh,' I smiled.

She just nodded the way a 2-year-old kid would react once he or she gots her favourite ice cream cone.

'One thing: please, please and please, never ever let Tamanna know that I refused the promotion,' I pleaded.

'I promise. Don't worry,' she assured me.

'By the way, how did Prashant know all this?' I doubted.

'Tushar told him,' she answered.

'How come...I mean...' I couldn't believe that Tushar divulged this when he promised me that he wouldn't.

'Well, do you remember when he enquired from you regarding your not getting the promotion letter and you had no answer?' she asked.

'Yes...so?'

'You know what he did afterwards? He went to Tushar's cabin and informed him what was going on between you and me, though he already knew what was brewing between us courtesy a few informers in the team. He even persuaded Tushar that a few veterans in the team kept on scoffing at the fact that you didn't receive any promotion and because of all that you were planning to put in your papers. Then Tushar told him what exactly happened that day,' she revealed.

'Later on he also assured Tushar that he would not let you resign,' she said.

I knew he'd become skeptical by my behaviour then, but to imagine that he would do something like that was beyond my imagination.

'What happened, Radhika? Why you were crying?' Tamanna asked solicitously.

'No…it's nothing,' she answered.

'Then…?' she asked.

'I'll tell you later. Let's go to the washroom,' Radhika answered as they walked towards the ladies washroom.

At first I felt like hurling my shoes at Prashant for lying in front of Tushar, but then it was him who cleared the air between me and Radhika so I decided to forgive everything.

For a change this time I hugged him tightly and lifted him. He just reciprocated.

How quickly the tables were turned. Just a few months back I'd sacrificed my promotion for my friendship, and that day Radhika did the same by not extending her shifts after getting aware of the truth which eventually helped me to win the competition. She was a true gem at heart. Winning the competition not only bridged the gap between our friendship but also acted as a lifesaver for my bedridden love.

Tamanna too was back to her usual self. The comparisons between Amit and me reduced after that. Maybe it was all her frustration at not seeing her boyfriend becoming a Team Leader that prodded her to indulge in that.

Party at Sanjay's House

It had been a week since I was declared winner of the Jack of All Trades contest, however I was still paying the price, I mean parties either in the cafe or at roadside dhabas. Though the monetary benefit was Rs. 10,000, I was sure I'd already spent at least half the winning amount. I observed that when it comes to parties even your enemies are at peace with you.

Although Sanjay was not my antagonist I preferred to keep a distance from him, Soon after I won the contest, I received an ST message from him.

'*Kya baat! Kya baat! Shiv,*' he wrote.

'Thanks, brother,' I replied.

'Let's arrange a party at my room. It will be only a boy's party,' he wrote.

'And if you people want I will arrange girls and don't worry, you don't have to pay anything,' He made a wicked smiley face.

'We shall take Ashok with us. The despo will pay for all of us. Do you agree?' he questioned.

'Thanks but no thanks, brother. You take Ashok along with you,' I wrote back.

He was calling Ashok a despo while the truth was that both of them were sex maniacs. The irony was that both of them were 'happily married', at least on paper.

I knew Sanjay was a hard ass who would never capitulate so easily. Instead, he preyed on the soft target, Prashant.

'Let's go for the party,' Prashant tried to persuade me.

'You know him and his intentions. He wants to invite call girls,' I whispered.

'Really!' he said, his eyes popping out.

'Just shut up. If Tamanna gets to know about all she'll slaughter me,' I murmured.

'OK. I have an idea,' Prashant said.

'What?'

'It will be a call girl–free party. Only booze and non-veg will be allowed,' he said.

'You are expecting an ass not to behave like an ass?' I asked.

'Come on. You have given a party to almost everyone on the floor. I will convince him not to invite any call girls,' he said.

'See, I just want to see Ashok's dance. You know how he dances. It will be fun,' he said.

Ashok had his own unique way of dancing, or say striking the dance floor. I myself didn't want to miss his dance at any cost but it was only after Prashant assured me that there wouldn't be any call girls that I agreed to join them.

Now the hard part was to convince Tamanna to give the green signal.

'They are all insisting on the party,' I said to Tamanna.

'I hope you people won't indulge in anything else other than drinks,' she said after a pause.

'What do you mean?' I innocently asked her.

'I mean call girls,' she said brusquely. I was not expecting her to be so direct.

'Are you mad?' I said.

'I know about Sanjay's character and his intentions,' she said.

'See, even I didn't want to go there in the first place, but at times you have to think about others too. It's only when Sanjay assured us there won't be anything like that, that I agreed,' I said.

'That's fine. I trust you.' She smiled. When your girlfriend says that she trusts you, it means a lot. You better stick to it otherwise you'd lose her forever.

We reached Sanjay's house in NOIDA Sector 50 sharp at 7 o'clock in the evening. As expected his wife had already left for her parents' home. At times I wondered how come his wife never doubted his flings with call girls. This guy really had balls of steel otherwise who would dare to call prostitutes in his own backyard.

Ashok had already reached before us. Sanjay informed us that Sandeep could not make it due to some last minute urgency. Not sure whether it was intentional or coincidental. The moment Ashok saw us he extended his hand for a handshake. With no other options I had to oblige. Prashant was saved because he was still wearing his driving gloves.

He decided to keep on his driving gloves the moment he saw Ashok. Bastard!

The first thing I did was to rush towards the washroom to wash my hands. As usual Ashok was clueless about the whole incident.

Soon I returned to his drawing room and relaxed on the sofa placed at a distance from Ashok.

'This one is for Shiv's success!' we all clicked our glasses together.

I had made up my mind that I wouldn't have more than one drink as my nightmare party was still fresh in my memory. In the true sense if one has to learn how to arrange a drink party, it has to be Sanjay. Four brands of beer, two brands of whisky, and to complement them he had arranged snacks like fried peanuts, potato chips, etc. Even though it was I who financed all that but the arrangements were commendable.

Sanjay excused himself on the pretext of arranging non veg snacks for us. Ashok on the other hand kept eating peanuts as if he wouldn't be getting anything else for dinner.

'I have something important to talk,' I said to Prashant while sipping my beer.

'What?' Prashant enquired.

I educated him about the comparison drawn by Tamanna between an auto rickshaw traveler (me) and a BMW owner (Amit).

'Don't know how to react. At times it really frustrates me a lot being compared to her ex-boyfriend. Is she in two minds or what?' I asked.

'What do you mean by "in two minds"?' he questioned, swirling the ice with his finger.

'Is it because I saved her that she thinks that it's her obligation to stay with me? At times I feel she really loves me, but the very next moment she acts differently.'

'I think you need to give her some time. You can't expect her to forget five years of a relationship in two months time,' he said.

Prashant had a valid point. It was my bad luck that Amit came in her life before me and stayed with her for almost five years. Even after his repeated attempts to woo her she didn't respond to any of his calls or SMS. It was sufficient to prove her loyalty towards me.

All of a sudden Sanjay's shrill voice intruded in my thoughts and brought me back to reality.

'Guys, I have a surprise for you all!' Sanjay proclaimed and clapped.

Two girls emerged from the adjacent room. No prizes for guessing, the kind of skimpy clothes and bright makeup they were wearing clearly suggested that they were call girls. Both of them were in their twenties and before we could react, they started shaking their hips to the music playing in the background.

It was the first time when apart from fried peanuts something else fascinated Ashok's attention. It's a common idiom that pretty girls make men's mouths water. I'm not sure about how pretty these girls were, but looking at Ashok's face, the theory turned out to be true. I could see him slowly strolling towards the girls. Soon he was shaking hands with them. It was the only time when I felt pity for the girls as they were oblivious of the filth behind those hands. He too started dancing along with the girls. It was excruciating to watch a hippopotamus jigging along with two deers.

'I *told* you not to do this! You promised me!' I was livid.

'Come on, it's just for fun,' Sanjay cajoled.

'No! I clearly told you about this and you *still* did it,' I charged.

'See? I told you an ass will remain an ass,' I ranted, looking at Prashant.

Surprisingly, he didn't respond. The fact that he refused to counter made me suspicious.

My outcry made the girls freeze on their feet, however it didn't deter Ashok's moves who continued to swing around the girls.

'Were you aware of this?' I questioned Prashant.

'Yes,' Sanjay grinned.

'Come on. How can you do this Prashant? It's like backstabbing,' I raised my hands in despair.

'What's wrong in having some fun till the time you do not end up in bed?' Prashant said, trying desperately to justify himself.

'You know very well how much I hate all this,' I said.

'To be honest now it's you and not Sanjay who has disappointed me the most.'

'I…I am really sorry Shiv. I didn't want to hurt you…' he lamented.

Before he could finish his sentence I said, 'I am leaving. If you want you can come with me.' Being my friend I wanted to give him one last opportunity to amend his mistake.

'Come on Shiv. Don't ruin the party. They are here for entertainment, brother,' he said.

'I think it's you and not me who has ruined the party, my friend,' I replied, tying my shoelaces.

Even though I had given Prashant an option to stay, he preferred to go with me as he didn't want to further infuriate me. The way he was tying his shoelaces at ultra-slow speed clearly showed his intense craving to stay there.

Except me everybody else was depressed but the person most affected by all was none other than Ashok. The very thought of a party (i.e. losing an opportunity to have sex) being over had devastated him. I could envisage him bursting into tears any moment.

Not sure what girls were thinking at the moment. They were standing in a corner with bewildered looks. One thing was definite that they hadn't met anyone who was least interested in sleeping with them.

'Could you please speed up?' I said sternly.

'Sh…sure. Just give me a minute,' Prashant answered as he walked towards the washroom.

'Come on Shiv. I promise I won't repeat it again,' Sanjay pleaded.

'I am sorry Sanjay. It's my fault that I trusted you,' I replied.

Suddenly Sanjay's cell phone rang. I didn't know what happened but he was quivering the moment he answered the call. His forehead broke into sweat all of a sudden. Something was terribly wrong I thought.

'N…now! H…how much time?' He was shuddering.

Before I could understand anything he threw his cell phone on the sofa and rushed towards the window.

'What happened Sanjay?' I enquired.

He didn't respond, instead he gazed out through the corner window. Not sure whether he was expecting anybody.

'Who is it?' Prashant enquired. I shrugged.

'M…my wife is standing outside,' he stammered.

'What? How come she's here?' I howled.

'You told us that your wife would be coming tomorrow,' Prashant said.

'I…I don't know. My life has ended now. No one can save me,' he cringed.

'I told you to stay away from all this but you didn't listen,' I hollered at Sanjay.

'Please save me brother. Do something!' he pleaded.

'Fuck you!' I screamed. Even though it was his house and his wife, but I too was present in the house along with two call girls. Nobody would believe my words that I was not cognizant of his fucking plan. I was sure that after Sanjay's wife caught him red-handed and kicked him out of her life, eventually everybody in the office would get to know of his wrongdoings, including Tamanna and Radhika. I was more bothered about Tamanna's reaction after she got to know about it. It would definitely be dreadful. Two things are definite if your girlfriend finds you with a call girl, either she'll stone you to death or leave you forever. I didn't want anything like that to happen, at least not when I was not even a part of their sexual intrigue though I was starving for sex for quite some time.

Ashok on the other hand burst into tears. I had never seen a wailing adult chimpanzee on Nat Geo or Discovery channels but I was convinced that it would look somewhat similar to Ashok. The girls were petrified by the sudden change of events.

His wife called in only after she reached home, and to top it all there was no back door in the house. We were trapped inside his house with no escape.

It was only Prashant who remained unruffled by all that. It appeared that he was pondering about all the possible options available at the moment.

'Can you do something? She will be here any moment,' I beseeched.

'I have an idea,' Prashant murmured.

'What?' we all chorused.

'I can save you but you have to make a promise.' He looked at Sanjay.

'I will do whatever you ask me. Just save me!' he begged.

When a company is on the verge of bankruptcy, the only option left for the employees is to accept what is being offered rather than to negotiate for a better deal. Sanjay's family life was on the verge of devastation and the only ray of hope left was Prashant's idea, so he had to agree to his demand.

'Going forward you will remain loyal to your wife only and no fucking around with call girls...' he threw the ball in his court.

'I promise!' he responded even before Prashant could complete his sentence.

A guy who used to brag about his sexual encounters almost every other day was ready to forfeit all that just to save his married life showed how vulnerable he was at the moment. Though I really wanted his wife to know about his real nature it would be an end game and that would be dreadful for his daughter. I wished that after this he'd be a changed man.

Once again Prashant attested that he was a true friend. The way he skillfully used the situation to straighten Sanjay's twisted life not only won my heart but also flushed out the resentment in me for not being informed about the call girls showing up in the party.

'Okay. Now here is the plan,' he said. We all focused on his words like obedient children.

'Sanjay, you will introduce all of us as your colleagues, including the girls. I hope you two know some English?' he enquired.

The girls first looked at each other's faces and then murmured, 'We…can do…try.'

Their bewildered expressions clearly stated that for them performing a striptease in front of strangers was a far easier task than to speak in English.

'OK. I will handle that. You two just keep mum,' he instructed.

'Quickly get your formal clothes on. I assume you brought them.'

'Yes we have,' the girls answered and rushed to the adjacent room to change their clothes.

'Sanjay, for God's sake behave normally, because if you falter then everything will be ruined. I'll take care of the rest,' he cautioned Sanjay.

Sanjay nodded.

As we settled on the couches within seconds somebody pressed the doorbell. Sanjay's wife was standing outside. Prashant animatedly asked Sanjay to open the door.

Sanjay limped towards the door to unlock it. In the meantime Ashok made the sign of the cross in the air. It's only in times of difficulty that you want every god irrespective of the religion you follow to bestow their blessings on you.

As per the plan the girls were seated besides me and Ashok was seated all alone in the corner.

'What's going on?' she raised the first question looking at us.

'I told you about the p…party, dear,' Sanjay replied.

'Hello *Bhabhi*. How are you?' Prashant greeted and flashed almost his entire front teeth.

'Hello *Bhabh*i. How are you?' We copied him. Prashant turned towards us and gave a scowl suggesting that we didn't need to copy every step of his.

'I…am fine,' she responded with a befuddled look on her face.

'Sorry *Bhabhi*. We had no other place so we forced Sanjay to organize it here,' he said in an apologetic tone.

'That's f…fine.' She smiled.

'Thanks *Bhabhi*. We are celebrating Shiv's success.' He pointed to me.

I grinned.

'Oh. Now I remember. Sanjay told me about it,' she said.

'Why don't you join us? I hope he won't mind.' Prashant gave a sheepish smile looking at Sanjay.

'No, no. You people carry on,' she replied.

'OK *Bhabhi*. Your wish is my command, but the next time you have to join us,' he smirked.

'OK. OK, sure,' she answered.

'By the way, meet Radhika and Tamanna. I hope Sanjay told you about them too.' He introduced the girls.

Even before she could respond he continued, 'Radhika is my girlfriend and Tamanna is Shiv's girlfriend.'

He could have referred to her as somebody else, like Ashok's wife, etc. I didn't care, but at least not Tamanna. I thought.

I couldn't even vent my anger and instead clutched the glass in my hand. I wished I could swap the glass with either Sanjay's or Ashok's neck.

'Girls, say hi to *Bhabhi*,' he instructed.

Both the girls waved their hands like well trained animals in circus.

'Oh. Hello girls,' Sanjay's wife acknowledged.

She excused herself and retired to the adjacent room. We all heaved a sigh as now the situation was under control.

'I'll kill you!' I muttered to Sanjay.

We stayed there for another 15 minutes and moved out on the pretext of dropping the girls at their residences as it was getting late.

Later on Prashant told me that he had no option but to introduce the girls because he sensed the growing suspicion on Sanjay's wife's face. He even apologized for referring to one of the call girls as Tamanna by holding both his ears.

I knew it was not intentional so I forgave him, After all he'd saved our asses and Sanjay's 'happy' married life.

The most important thing that happened post that day was Sanjay's surprisingly changed behaviour. I didn't expect such a turnaround from a guy like him, but the trauma he went through made the impossible possible.

The only question which his wife frequently asked was how come our girlfriends had applied gaudy make up and were wearing such high-heeled sandals. As per her it looked so cheap.

The only thing I could reply was that she didn't notice their ultra-revealing dresses otherwise only God knew what would have happened that day.

The Call from New York

It took some time to acclimatize myself being in a relationship with a girl who had an ex-boyfriend. Earlier I used to get peeved by constant comparison but gradually I made peace with myself. I had comprehended that if tomorrow God forbid I got into a relationship with some other girl, I would also do the same. It would be impossible to expunge Tamanna from my memory, so how could I expect her to obliterate her past with Amit?

'What does the future hold for us here?' I questioned Radhika who was busy applying nail polish.

It seems that females know about males' attraction for the colour red. It can more easily incite sexual feelings when compared to other colours. Even in the majority of porn movies I had seen that the females prefer red over other colours.

'To be honest I don't know,' she replied, blowing on her nails.

'Don't know? You know what, yesterday I came to know that one of the processes is getting rammed down and most of the associates are about to lose their jobs,' I said dejectedly.

'Yeah I know that. It's atrocious,' she said as if it was not a big deal. She continued with applying nail polish on her other hand.

'But how can they do this? There's one guy who comes in my cab who has been asked to look out for a job. He has been given two months notice period only.' I was baffled.

'Come on. You are not a school kid so don't talk like one. It's a business and not a charity for them, and if they are not able to earn profit then please elucidate why should they keep you?' she asked.

Her tone was firm. It was the first time she looked straight leaving her index finger half painted.

'…but the guy has a family to support,' I murmured.

'Don't be an emotional fool. He will hunt for another job,' she answered.

'So does it mean it might happen with us as well?'

'No, you are the company CEO's would-be son-in-law. They won't fire you,' she mocked.

'Don't talk rubbish. The day Americans decide to pull back their jobs, we'll all be jobless,' she continued.

'You know, I never thought like this before,' I said innocently.

'Now I'm really worried about my future with Tamanna,' I said.

'Yes. You need to.' She smirked as she rose to her feet, which meant that now it was the turn of her toes to get glossed. Why can't females do all this stuff at home? 'Have you ever seen a male shaving on the floor?' I thought. It was really annoying to hold her bottle of nail polish.

'Let me tell you about a call from New York City which still haunts me sometimes in my dreams,' she said.

'I got this call from a lady. I still remember her name was Cheryl. As usual I parroted my introductory lines, but you know what she said after that?' she asked.

'What?' I asked.

'She lost her job because her job was outsourced to some call centre in India. She was a single mother and desperately needed a job to take care of her baby,' she said in a trembling voice.

'Then?' I asked inquisitively.

'I was frozen as I didn't expect something like that. Suddenly she broke down on the call,' she said.

'Even though I wanted to speak I couldn't. I felt as if somebody had tied my tongue. It was the only time when I had to transfer the call to my supervisor in the US,' she continued.

'That day I sobbed like a newborn in the washroom. That day I realized how guilty I was in taking somebody else's job. I was sure that one day God would definitely chastise for my sins.' She sighed.

However at that moment she didn't have any remorse as she continued with her task of nail painting.

I got jittery after getting aware of the callous reality of a BPO.

This job could go at any moment. The moment Americans see their expenses inflating or profits receding, they'll pull back their jobs. If they could do this with their own people then it's ludicrous to expect leniency for us. 'Is this one of the reasons why we don't get respect from our own society?' I thought.

'Our job is like a time bomb. We all know that it will explode one day, but it's just the timing we are not sure of,' she said, closing the bottle. At last the job of nail painting had been done.

Only in the movies can a hero live a happy life with plenty of love and less money but in real life it's just opposite. We can survive with less love but need loads of money.

There were other issues apart from this which I shut my eyes to before falling in love with Tamanna. I was on the wrong side of 20 and that too a general category candidate. It meant that I had hardly a couple of years left to apply for any government jobs as the upper age limit for almost all the jobs was only 30.

To envisage myself studying and clearing the entrance test was a distant mirage in the middle of the Sahara desert and that too after spending almost 12–13 hours daily in office.

I should have continued with my CA studies, at least then I would have got some respectable job, I repented.

To have a job and not a girlfriend is still tolerable, but a girlfriend without a job is a torment. I was going crazy. It would be a tough nut to crack another job in a BPO sector. I still had memories of how much I had to go through before securing this job.

Tamanna sacrificed a BMW to be with an auto rickshaw, and in return I couldn't even guarantee her a decent life. This thought was killing me.

I was desperate to find a solution but didn't know where to begin.

'Hi Mama. How are you? Missing me?' SMS from Tamanna.

She was on leave that day as she had to go along for her room partner's bridal shopping who was getting married soon. No prizes for guessing that her bridegroom was an engineer with an IT company based in the US.

'Yes *mera bachha*. I am fine. Missing you,' I replied.

Throughout the day I'd build castles in the air to secure my future with Tamanna but at last came to the conclusion that even with all my best efforts and good luck I could only upgrade myself from an auto rickshaw traveller to either a Zen or an Alto owner, but certainly not a BMW owner.

'Is everything all right? You look tense?' Tamanna enquired looking at my sullen face in the cafe the following day.

'No…nothing,' I hesitated.

'I can see something is bothering you. Please tell me,' she appealed squeezing my hand.

'Are you aware of the process which is ramming down?' I asked.

She nodded.

'And because of it many of the associates have been asked to look for alternatives,' I continued.

'It's awful,' she said.

'This might happen with us too,' I hinted.

'OK, now I got it. Don't worry my dear, we shall be able to manage.' She smiled.

'I don't need a bungalow. I will be content with a two-room set.' She chuckled, caressing my hand.

I could only smile, but somewhere I knew without job it would be extremely difficult to run even a two-room set flat, leave alone a bungalow.

I started to explore the options available for me. Apart from studies I used to draw when I was growing up. But thanks to my Dad I had to give up. I still remember the day when I told him that I wanted to be a painter. My father asked me a question with the precondition that if I failed to answer I would do what he wanted me to do.

He asked me to name any five famous Indian painters. As expected apart from M F Husain I still depended on Google for another four names. It's been ages since I last drew something. It was one of my childhood dreams, though my foremost dream was to join a circus. As a child I used to get mesmerized by their performance, especially of the girls. Till date I had never seen so many beautiful girls showing up at one place other than at a circus. I used to cry when I had to go back home. My parents literally had to drag me out of the circus tent after the show. I was determined as a child to join the circus once I grew up.

Fortunately I didn't join the circus, but ironically my life had become a circus. I was frantically trying to keep my balance on a thin rope tied between my professional and love lives.

I used to write short stories for my school magazine but to fantasize myself as the next Chetan Bhagat was beyond my wildest dream. He was an ex-IITian along with ex-IIMian, and I had failed thrice in my CA exams. Seriously, there was no comparison between the two of us.

'How to become a millionaire,' I typed in the 'most loved' words in Google search.

Though I knew it was one of the most ludicrous things to do but when your future looks wobbly even absurd things start making some sense. Even though I got more than a hundred thousand results in less than a second none of them seemed realistic. Some talked about following some seven steps while others talked about ridiculous things like planning a bank robbery or getting married to some millionaire's daughter. Well, one needs to have balls of steel to carry out a bank robbery or Hritik Roshan's looks to impress a millionaire's daughter; sadly I didn't possess any of those qualities.

I wished that just by typing in the desired words, Google could make that a reality like a genie in a bottle but I knew my wish would always remain a wish.

Another week passed by without any success.

Every day when the shift ended it was my duty to look for Tamanna's cab parked next to the company's boundary wall. Even though it was impossible that an alluring girl would ever miss her cab, I ensured to locate her cab before anyone else. In order to score some brownie points, there would a despo cab mate who would make sure to give a call or if required might also lie down in front to forestall the cab from departing. Nobody bothers if a guy has boarded the cab or not.

It was a tedious job to search for her cab when the street lights were turned off. There wasn't much of a crowd outside, yet we had came out a bit early to have tea outside.

'There you go Tamanna,' I cheered the moment I saw her route number placed on a cab.

As I turned towards her I could see someone approaching towards her from behind. His face was not visible due to the dusk.

First I thought he was some other employee who too was looking for his cab, but then he grabbed Tamanna's shoulders with his hands.

Before I could reciprocate, I heard Tamanna, 'What are you doing here?'

'Just go from here Amit. Don't create a scene here!' she yelped, releasing herself from his grip.

'What the fuck is he doing here?' I thought.

'Please forgive me. I just want you back in my life,' he implored.

'Just leave Amit. People are looking at us,' she yelled.

At present more than 'people' it was me who mattered the most for her.

'I am sorry, but please don't leave me. I just can't live without you.' He was tearful.

I was dumbfounded and didn't know how to react.

'It's over between us. I have someone else who saved my life from hooligans and loves me like anything. I can't jilt him,' she said.

It made my chest inflate with pride. I wished I could let people know that the person she just talked about was none but me.

All of a sudden Amit simmered down. He just stood there for another minute as he stared at Tamanna. Then he wiped his tears and slowly shuffled away without uttering another word.

Even though he was Tamanna's ex-boyfriend and whatever he did was inappropriate I still felt sorry for him.

As expected Tamanna broke into tears as other females rushed to soothe her. I didn't feel like talking to her in front of the whole world so I decided to walk away from there.

'Please take care of her,' I asked one of her cab mates and left the scene.

As I was strolling towards my cab somebody patted me on my shoulder. It was Sanjay.

'Where's that motherfucker? How dare he touch you? I'll kill him!' he grunted.

'Relax. It's over now. He's already left,' I replied.

'There was some misunderstanding. Now it has been cleared so no need to lose your nerves,' I tried to camouflage the real incident.

However it was evident that this would become a hot topic to scuttlebutt tomorrow in the We Guest campus.

She kept on calling me the whole time but I didn't pick her call.

'I am not angry. It's just that I am feeling a bit sleepy. Will talk to you tomorrow,' I sent an SMS the moment I reached home.

'It's not my fault Mama. I didn't know he would come to office and misbehave. I am really sorry' she wrote back.

'No need to say sorry. I know it was not your fault. I just need some time,' I replied.

'Please Mama please. Just talk to me once otherwise I won't be able to sleep ☹' she wrote.

It was an emotional blackmailing SMS from her. Females use this weapon of 'male self-esteem destruction' when all other tricks fall flat. With no options left I called her.

'I am really sorry Mama,' she blubbered.

'Please Tamanna, calm down. I know it was not your fault,' I appealed.

'First swear on me that you're not angry,' she demanded.

'I swear I'm not at all angry.'

'OK Mama. This is what I wanted to know. Now if you want you can sleep.' She was elated.

'OK. Will call you tomorrow,' I said.

'OK Mama. Will wait for your call. Sweet dreams,' she said as we disconnected. I avoided discussing Amit's fracas outside the company's premises as it could further distress her.

In no time I received an SMS from Tamanna. 'Thanks Mama. Love U ☺'

I didn't reply instead kept my mobile on the table and collapsed on my bed.

However I couldn't sleep as I kept on tossing and turning throughout the day. There were so many things right from job security to the stupid scene that were responsible for my lack of sleep. It turned out to be one of the most miserable days of my entire life so far.

Next day everyone in the campus was busy yakking about the previous night's incident without even knowing what actually had happened there. It's the feeling of joy or pleasure when one sees another fail or suffer misfortune. In the gossip world people have a tendency to append their own versions to further spice up the real incident. Later I got to know from Prashant that stories like a guy tried to grope Tamanna from behind, her ex-boyfriend tried to batter me and so on. Some tried to pry but I evaded answering them. Some people just get a thrill from spreading derogatory stories about others.

It might be that some people are idle; with nothing constructive to do so they indulge in slandering other's images. Fucking losers.

A week passed by however there was no end to the rumours and it started to show up in my calls. As usual I quietly logged on my system and made myself available for calls. Almost immediately my Avaya phone blinked. I pressed the answering button.

'Thank you for calling Finger House. This is Scott. How may I help you?' I opened my call.

'Where are you located?' the caller petulantly enquired.

'Your call has been transferred to India,' I answered reluctantly.

'You fucking asshole. I want to talk to somebody American not you filthy Indian,' he ranted.

Even though I was accustomed to such bashing but that time I had no idea what triggered me to retort.

'You faggot ass. Just fuck off if you don't want to talk to an Indian.' I vented all my frustrations on the poor customer.

My voice was loud and everyone around me craned their necks towards me. I instantly disconnected the call and stomped out.

The customer must be cursing the time he decided to give me a call. It spread like a fire in the wild and as expected I was soon summoned inside Tushar's cabin for explanation of my on-call behaviour.

'Do you know what you did?' he questioned. For the first time his tone was unsympathetic.

I didn't reply.

'You know what you did? You have not only risked your own job but also jeopardized the entire process!' he yelled.

'Shiv! I need an explanation!' He banged his fist on the table.

I got jittery.

For the first time anybody—and unfortunately it was me—saw his vicious side. He was trembling with anger.

'He was abusing me for no reasons. I just couldn't control my emotions on the call,' I muttered.

'Is it for the first time you were ill-treated for no reason? I am sure the answer is no. Being old in the system, I didn't expect this from you. You know you were about to get promotion and you have ruined everything,' he said dejectedly.

I didn't utter a word.

'It's a serious offence on your part. Do you know that?' he questioned.

I just nodded in response.

'You need to give me in writing that you won't repeat anything like this in future,' he said.

'Did you get that?' he growled.

'I…am sorry Sir, but it was not my fault,' I mumbled.

'I was bloody assisting him and he started reviling me. I…am sorry Sir but I won't write any apology mail,' I continued.

'What? Are you out of your mind?' He was stumped by my response.

'I won't apologize,' I was adamant.

He couldn't believe his ears as he scratched his forehead. After pondering over the limited options left at his disposal he finally spoke.

'Then you will have to resign, Shiv.'

'OK Sir,' I replied and made an exit from his cabin to leave him with some unrequited questions.

At My Workstation

I was encircled by my well-wishers.

'What happened?' Tamanna enquired.

'They want me to give in writing that nothing like this will happen again,' I said, frustrated.

Thank God,' Prashant heaved a sigh.

'So then write an apology,' Tamanna said.

'I won't,' I retorted as I clicked on New Message option.

'What the fuck are you talking? If it was someone else he would have been fired by now,' Radhika said.

'I have not done anything wrong so I won't say sorry.' I was obstinate.

'What about us then?' Tamanna murmured.

I didn't reply as I typed my resignation letter.

'Please take your resignation back,' Prashant appealed.

'No way.'

'Please don't write it for my sake. I want you to be here,' Tamanna pleaded.

I avoided looking at her face as tears started to flow down her cheeks.

'No I won't. I thought at least you would support me when others are abandoning me,' I said.

'Am I not supporting you? I just want you to act sensibly.'

'Please for God's sake just shut up. It all happened because of you and your fucking boyfriend Amit,' I almost screamed.

It added fuel to the fire as her sobbing intensified. Before I could say anything she rushed off the floor.

'Shiv, you have gone mad,' Radhika chided and walked out to console Tamanna.

Now it was Prashant's turn to rebuke me for my insensitivity. However he didn't say anything as I anticipated instead he too followed the girls.

'Shit!' I banged my fist on my workstation. All eyes on the floor swung towards me.

I promptly composed myself and continued to type the resignation letter.

It turned out to be my last day in We Guest.

When I joined the company I never dreamt that my end would be like this, but that's what you call destiny.

It also turned out to be the last day when I spoke to any of the three people whom I met in We Guest. My friends Prashant and Radhika and the most important person, the love of my life, Tamanna.

The way Prashant looked at me while stomping away from me denoted that there was no bigger loser in the world than me.

Somewhere in my heart I knew he was right.

Life Goes On

'Hello,' somebody addressed me.

'Hello! I am talking to you.' He snapped his finger to get my attention.

'H…huh!' I said as my eyes roved around.

'Just a moment ago I'd banged my fist on my workstation, so how come I reached here? Was I daydreaming?' I thought.

'Hello Sir, where are you lost?' He shook me with both hands.

'Oh…nothing. It's just that I fell asleep,' I murmured as reality checked in.

'You are here for your full and final settlement, right?' he enquired.

'Oh yes,' I replied wriggling my body.

'I am sorry for the delay but it was all my cab's fault. It brought me late.' He grinned.

'That's fine. I know about that,' I replied as I sat in front of him.

He started to search for my full and final settlement papers. After a few minutes he found them.

'Here you go Shiv,' he said.

'Your last day in office was 6th September 2009?' he questioned.

'Y…yes, it was,' I replied.

It's ironic that you may not recall your best days in life, but howsoever hard you may try you can't forget your bad days.

'OK. Here is your full and final settlement letter along with the settlement check.' He passed over the letter to me.

My heart sank the moment I saw the amount mentioned on the check. My expectation was much higher than the amount mentioned on the paper.

'What happened?' he asked looking at my anxious face.

'I was expecting a bit more than this,' I said.

'The explanation is written below. Kindly go through it,' He instructed.

I meticulously read the explanation written below. It stated that because I had not completed my notice period, a certain amount had been deducted from the overall compensation.

What the fuck, I thought.

I was asked to resign then how could I serve my notice period? There was some mix-up. Was it Tushar who didn't inform the HR to waive off my notice period clause or did HR do all the goof ups? I had full faith in Tushar who always did his bit to save my ass whenever I was in trouble but I wasn't sure about the HR there. I didn't want to spend another day to get the clarification so I decided to accept whatever was mentioned on the check.

'Is it OK now<' he asked.

I felt like giving him one tight slap then and there but somehow managed to control myself.

'Yes.'

There was no point arguing with him so I signed the acknowledgement paper and stomped out. I even ignored his handshake.

While climbing up the stairs I contemplated about all the sacrifices I made for the company, whether it was about extending my shift because of a huge inflow of calls or to even cancel my holidays for emergency requirements but it all seemed squandered today.

Somehow I was feeling betrayed while coming out of the campus.

I wanted to leave the premises before any familiar face recognized me. It was my good luck that even the full and final settlement guy was a new hiree.

As I was pacing towards the bus stand, somebody patted on my back.

To my horror it was Radhika standing there gasping for breath looking as if she'd just finished a 100-metres race.

The first thing she did after composing herself was to slap me without realizing that we were standing on a busy road with people around. Nobody had ever slapped me the way she did. It shook my jaw.

We were encircled by a few commuters who thought I was pestering her. If she hadn't intervened I'd have been thrashed within minutes.

'Where the fuck have you been?' she howled.

'Let's go from here. People are watching us,' I protested.

'I don't care. Answer me!'

'I'll answer all your queries but please let's move away from here,' I pleaded.

She realized it was not the right place to ask for answers so we decided to go to Bikaner restaurant on the opposite side of the road.

'Do you know how many times we tried to contact you be it on your mobile or on Orkut but not a single response?' she said, infuriated.

'I know,' I muttered.

'No you don't. If you knew you would have responded to at least one of the messages but you didn't care.' I could see tears rolling down her cheeks.

'I...am really sorry,' I whispered.

'No you're not. What the fuck do you think of yourself?' she yelled.

'Shhh!' I requested.

'Calm down Radhika. I'll answer all your queries.'

'You wanted to know why I did all that. I did it for Tamanna,' I said.

'What?' she said, shocked.

'Let me start from the beginning. You know how much I had to go through before securing this job. The day I got my appointment letter was one of the best days of my life and to complement that I got Tamanna as my girlfriend. I was over the moon the day she hugged me when I accidently saved her life from those hooligans. I thought my life had become complete and I didn't need anything else in life. But one key thing which we all overlooked was that she was going through a bad patch in her love life at that time and I was fortunate to reap the benefits of it. Even though she was loyal towards me but it was Amit who was her first love and not me,' I said.

Radhika was all attentive towards what I was saying.

'At the beginning she might have thought that she got someone who could replace Amit, but later on she started to miss him badly and that's when the comparisons started. Somewhere I felt she was forcing herself to stay with me because I'd saved her life. As I was trying to cope, another catastrophe struck in the form of the process being rammed down and people losing their jobs,' I continued.

'I started to panic as I didn't know what I would do without a job. Before I could figure out what else I could do apart from this job, Amit's scene happened outside the campus,' I said.

'After Amit's incident I couldn't sleep the whole day. I didn't know who was at fault, Tamanna, Amit or me. May be it was the circumstances which should be blamed for our misery. Too many things happened during that short time and it all made me anxious. I didn't know what to do,' I said.

'So you were afraid of your future, you coward? You surrendered even before trying?' she asked after pausing for a minute.

'If you want you may say that. At one point I was worried about the job, but when you compare my job with anybody else's in the company, mine was more secure for obvious reasons. It did bother me for quite some time, but that was not the primary reason for my leaving the company,' I said.

'Then why did you leave the company?' she asked in frustration.

'I was desperate to meet Amit in person after the logout incident. The way Amit begged in front of Tamanna made me realize how much he loved her. It was killing me so I wanted to know what was going in his heart. I am sure there is no dearth of beautiful girls for a BMW owner, but he only wanted Tamanna in his life, so I called him and set up a meeting in Ansal Plaza after two days,' I said.

'You called in your girlfriend's ex-boyfriend to meet?' she asked, shocked.

'Yes. I thought him to be like any other rich arrogant brat but surprisingly he was quite sober. After conversing for half an hour I realized how much he was missing Tamanna in his life and it really proved his love for her. He was trying to control his emotions but couldn't, and trust me it was all genuine. He even stated that he could do anything to get her back in his life and would never hurt her again,' I continued.

'Later it made me realize how much of a misfit I was between the two and then decided that it was my responsibility to amend what I did. The only way I could isolate myself from her was by quitting the job,' I said.

'…so I consciously scolded the poor customer that day and you know what happened afterwards,' I said.

Radhika was mum as tears kept rolling down her cheeks.

'Tamanna was the call of my life, but I had to let that call go away. She was the call which I would miss all my life,' I completed.

'But why the hell didn't you contact us?' she asked, sobbing.

'The reason I didn't was because I was sure one of you would find out the reality sooner or later and let know Tamanna of it,' I replied.

'By the way how is Prashant? Any plans of you two getting married?' I asked.

'It took some time for him to get used to your absence but now he is fine,' she said.

'That's good.'

'And no marriage plans for at least the next three–four years. Will decide after that,' she replied.

Though I was dying to know about Tamanna's wellbeing I didn't know how to begin. Radhika anticipated my inhibition.

'I have a bad news for you Shiv,' she whispered. Her tone was grave.

'What?' I said.

'Tamanna resigned the following week after you put in your papers. She too stopped taking our calls after that. It's recently we got to know that she was getting m…married next week,' she muttered.

I wished I could become deaf. I was expecting something like this coming my way but to actually get a confirmation was beyond my imagination. It's like doctor diagnosing last stage cancer and the only thing you could do was to linger on with no chances of survival. It was a terrible feeling.

I tried hard to control my tears but couldn't do that: even they wanted to show the world how cursed I was that day. Seeing me Radhika too started weeping.

It's only when the waiter intervened to enquire whether everything was all right that we stopped.

'It's getting late for your shift,' I said, wiping my tears.

'It's fine. I'll extend my shift,' She whispered.

'I want you to promise me something,' I said.

'What?'

'I told you everything because I trust you, but nobody, not even Prashant should know the truth,' I said.

'But why?' She was annoyed.

'Because I want it. Everyone's life is back on track, whether it's Tamanna or Prashant, and now I don't want any interruption because of me,' I replied.

'I promise,' she murmured after a minute's silence.

Soon it was time to leave.

'You know what, asshole. I have started to respect you a lot.' She smiled and hugged me.

'Me too dear,' I replied. I could feel her tears on my T-shirt.

I was not sure when I would meet her or Prashant again, but this world is a small place to live in and our industry was even smaller, so you never knew when we'd cross each other's paths.

As for Tamanna she would always remain my first love and even God could not change that fact.

I looked towards We Guest for one last time, a place where I had spent some of the best days of my life. They shall always remain a part of my life till my last breath.

'NOIDA, NOIDA, NOIDA!' I heard a man shouting his lungs out. His entire body was hanging outside the moving bus. Even Akshay Kumar would refrain from doing such stunts in any of his movies. I'd even shifted from Shakarpur to NOIDA so that nobody could trace me.

As I plunged towards the bus I could feel as if a heavy burden had been lifted off my shoulders in terms of friendship, but wasn't sure whether I'd ever get rid of the burden of love off my heart.

Life After We Guest

Surprisingly there wasn't much of a crowd in the bus; it even had a few vacant seats one of which I grabbed. The heartbreaking news of Tamanna's marriage made me overlook that the seat was reserved for ladies only. Though I was tearful somewhere I was content that she had moved on in her personal life and soon would become someone else's life. All of a sudden, a sweet voice interrupted my inner conflict.

'Excuse me, this seat is for ladies,' somebody murmured.

I looked up above the window, where it was clearly stated 'Reserved for ladies'. I just stood up without uttering a word. I didn't even look at the female who'd enlightened me.

Seeing my dejected face she offered. 'If you want you can...'

'No. It's fine. Please,' I interrupted before she could complete.

By now all the empty seats were occupied so the only option left was to remain standing till I reached my destination.

'If you want I may hold your bag,' the girl offered.

'Thanks,' I replied.

For the first time I saw her face while passing my bag to her. That very moment the driver abruptly applied the brakes. I stumbled on her but somehow managed to seize the seat's iron bar at the last moment.

'S…sorry!' I said.

'It's fine,' she smiled.

At first I was flabbergasted to see her face as it resembled Tamanna's a lot. The only difference between the two was the colour of the eyes and the complexion of the skin. Tamanna had big brown eyes while this girl had light blue eyes. Tamanna was fairer than this female. She was wearing a white *kurta* pajamas and was looking quite pretty in it. The perfectly placed little black *bindi* on her forehead enhanced her elegance.

I really don't know why God suddenly decided to play tricks with me. To divert my own attention I turned to the opposite direction.

But this time God too was ready: the lady seated next to her suddenly decided to get down on the next stop.

'Hey, you may sit here,' she said, tapping on my shoulder.

Even though I didn't feel like sitting next to her, I still took the seat as it would take at least another 30–40 minutes to reach my destination. I avoided eye contact with her so concentrated looking outside the window.

I'd decided that after departing from We Guest I'd go directly to my new company which was located in NOIDA itself as my shift was about to start. I had joined another BPO company and this time I got the job in my very first attempt. Thank God for that.

'I might have kept my company's ID in the bag. I better check,' I thought.

As I pulled out my company's ID the girl seated next to me enquired on seeing my ID card.

'Are you working with Nth Technologies?'

'Yes,' I answered unenthusiastically.

'What a coincidence. I have an interview scheduled there.' She smiled.

I kept silent. Now I was regretting my decision to look out for my ID card in the bag. But they say without God's will, not even a leaf can flutter. So it was an act of God that planned our meeting and that too on a day when I was crestfallen by the news of Tamanna's wedding. Not sure whether it was an indication of beginning of a new phase in my life or something else, only time would tell. I decided to leave everything on God to decide.

'Hi. My name is Vandana, and you?' she introduced herself, extending her hand. She wore silver coloured bangles which were making her arms appear slender.

'Hello. I'm Shiv,' I replied and shook her hand. A current passed through my arm.